The Enchanting World of Fairy Tales

Illustrated by Eric Kincaid

Designed and re-told by Desmond Marwood

CONTENTS

Brown Watson

ENGLAND

© 2004 Brown Watson, England

Reprinted 2004, 2005 (twice), 2006 (twice), 2007, 2011

Printed in Malaysia

The Princess and the Pea

A prince had travelled the world, looking for a princess to be his wife. 'Not one he has found seems to be a true princess,' said his mother, the queen. 'I understand,' she said, 'that a true princess has a very delicate sense of feeling!'

That night, a terrible storm broke out. There came a knocking at the palace door, so loud that the king went to see who it was. 'Yes?' he called. 'Who is there?'
'A princess, seeking shelter!' came a voice. She did not look like a princess. Rain trickled down her face and she was soaked to the skin.

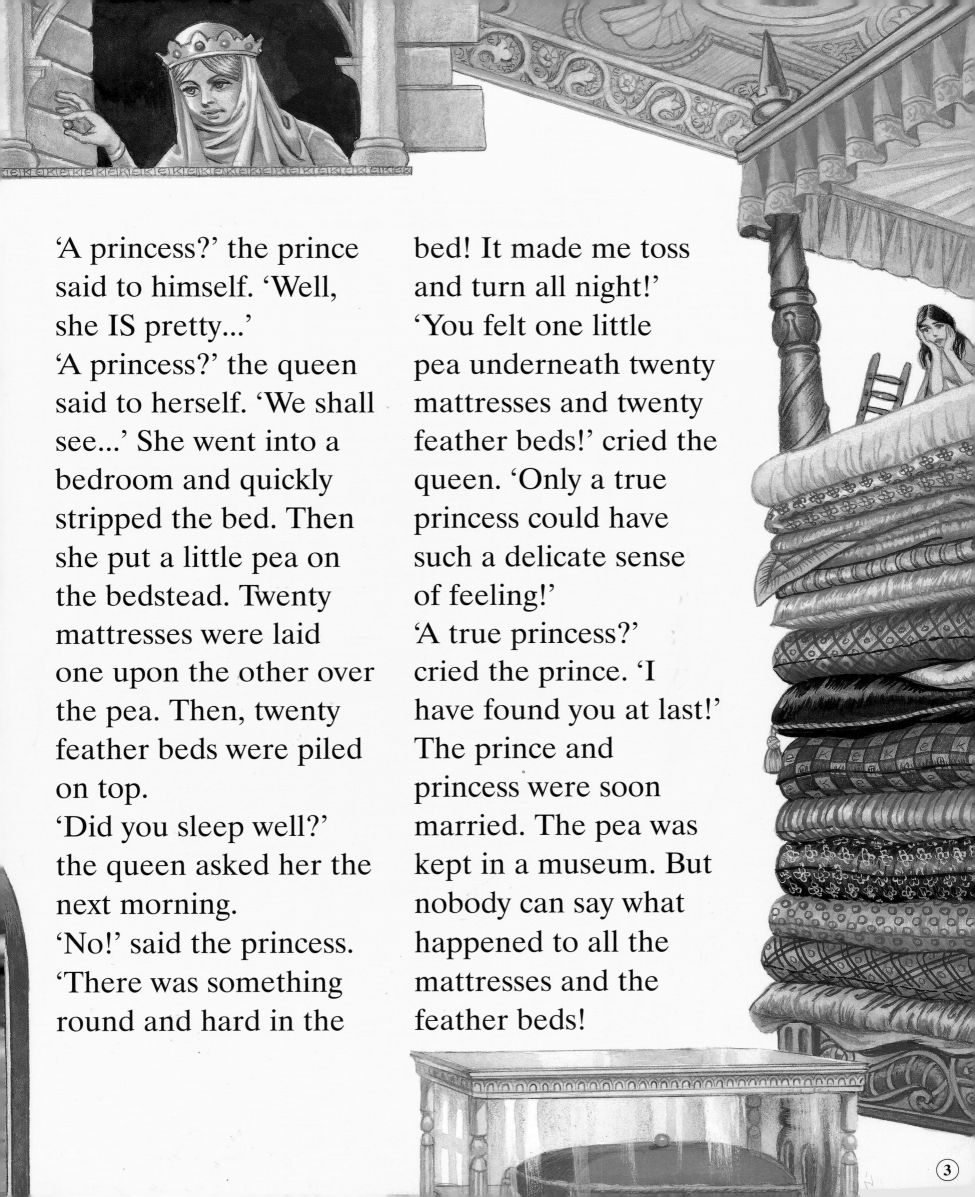

'A princess?' the prince said to himself. 'Well, she IS pretty...'

'A princess?' the queen said to herself. 'We shall see...' She went into a bedroom and quickly stripped the bed. Then she put a little pea on the bedstead. Twenty mattresses were laid one upon the other over the pea. Then, twenty feather beds were piled on top.

'Did you sleep well?' the queen asked her the next morning.

'No!' said the princess. 'There was something round and hard in the bed! It made me toss and turn all night!'

'You felt one little pea underneath twenty mattresses and twenty feather beds!' cried the queen. 'Only a true princess could have such a delicate sense of feeling!'

'A true princess?' cried the prince. 'I have found you at last!' The prince and princess were soon married. The pea was kept in a museum. But nobody can say what happened to all the mattresses and the feather beds!

Sleeping Beauty

There was great rejoicing in the kingdom when the King and Queen had a baby daughter. All the fairies in the land were among those invited to a banquet at the royal palace. They all wanted to celebrate the arrival of the new baby princess. All the fairies that is, except one, who was the well-known Wicked Fairy. So, she invited herself to the banquet. "I'm sure you didn't mean to leave me out, did you?" she smiled sweetly at the King. "Oh, dear me no!" said the King, hoping to keep the Wicked Fairy happy. "Please do sit down and enjoy yourself. I'm so glad you came."

The Wicked Fairy sat down muttering. "They're happy now, but I'll soon change that!"

One of the Good Fairies heard what
she said and quickly hid herself. She
wanted to make sure the Wicked Fairy
did not try to harm the baby princess in any way.
After the banquet, each fairy blessed the baby
with a magical gift such as wisdom, beauty and
music. Soon, only the Wicked Fairy was left –
or so she thought! She did not know that
the Good Fairy was still hiding away!
The Wicked Fairy leaned over the
baby sleeping in her royal cradle.
"My gift to you is doom!"
she screamed out loud.

"I say," cried the Wicked Fairy, "that if this princess ever pricks her finger on a spindle while working at a spinning wheel, she will die!" Then, the Wicked Fairy vanished in a cloud of black smoke. The King and Queen and all their subjects were worried because there were spinning wheels and spindles in every home in the land. Every girl, even a princess, was taught how to spin the wool from sheep and almost all pricked their finger on the spindle at some time or other.

Then, the Good Fairy came out from her hiding place to give the Princess her gift. "I do not have the power to break the spell of the Wicked Fairy," she said, "but I can change it. If the princess does prick her finger on a spindle, she will not die. Instead, she will fall into a deep sleep. She will only wake if she is kissed by a person who truly loves her. That is the best that I can promise."

Princess Petal, as she became known,
grew up to be beautiful and wise. She
had all the good qualities bestowed upon her
by the Good Fairies when she was a baby.
Her father, the King, did all in his power to protect her
and all the spindles in the land were destroyed. Life seemed
safe and the Wicked Fairy's spell was almost forgotten.
Then, one day, the princess found a part of the
old palace she had never explored before. At the
top of a staircase, in a tiny room, was an old
woman spinning wool – and using a spindle!
"May I see that," asked Princess Petal and
as she took the spindle, its sharp point
pricked her finger. The princess
collapsed immediately.

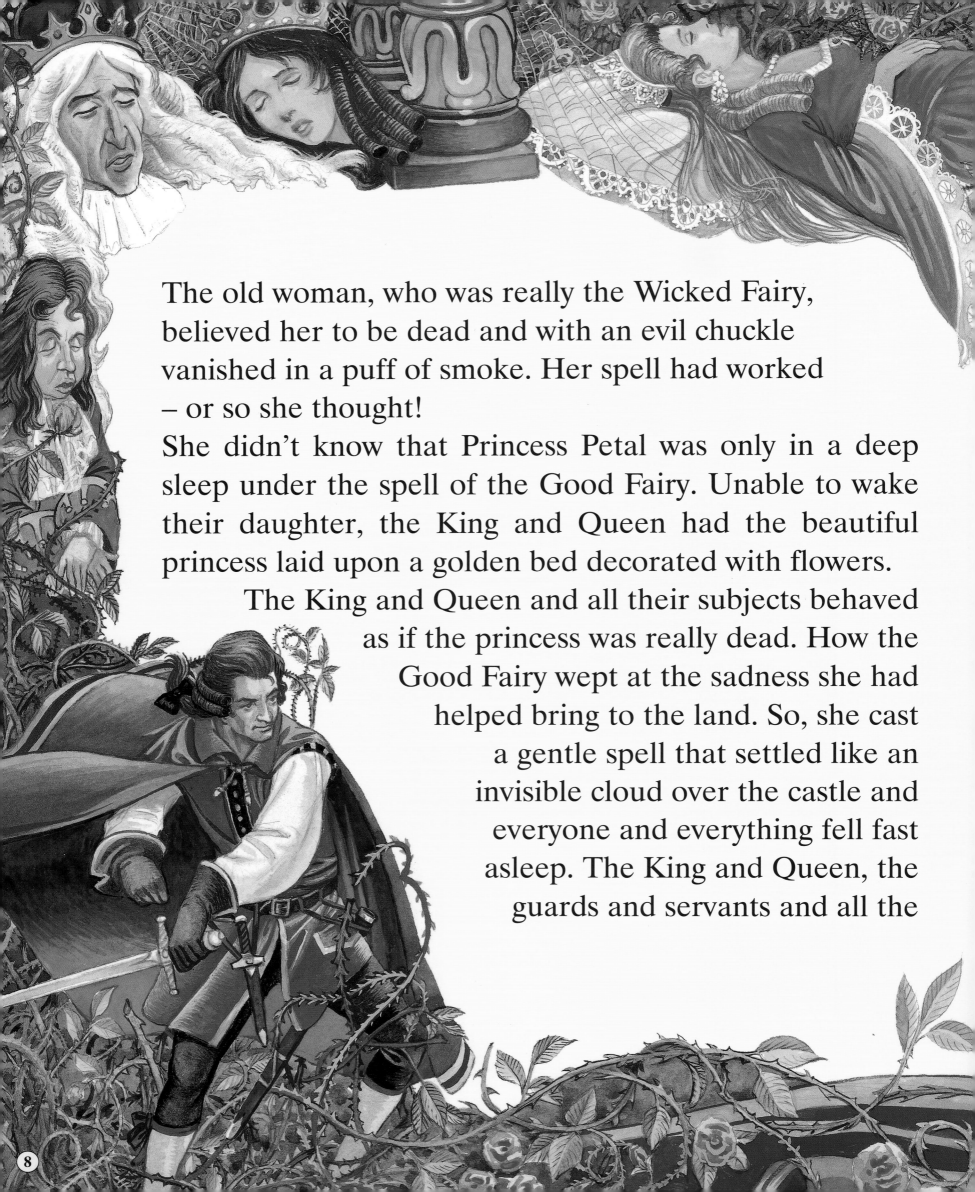

The old woman, who was really the Wicked Fairy, believed her to be dead and with an evil chuckle vanished in a puff of smoke. Her spell had worked – or so she thought!

She didn't know that Princess Petal was only in a deep sleep under the spell of the Good Fairy. Unable to wake their daughter, the King and Queen had the beautiful princess laid upon a golden bed decorated with flowers.

The King and Queen and all their subjects behaved as if the princess was really dead. How the Good Fairy wept at the sadness she had helped bring to the land. So, she cast a gentle spell that settled like an invisible cloud over the castle and everyone and everything fell fast asleep. The King and Queen, the guards and servants and all the

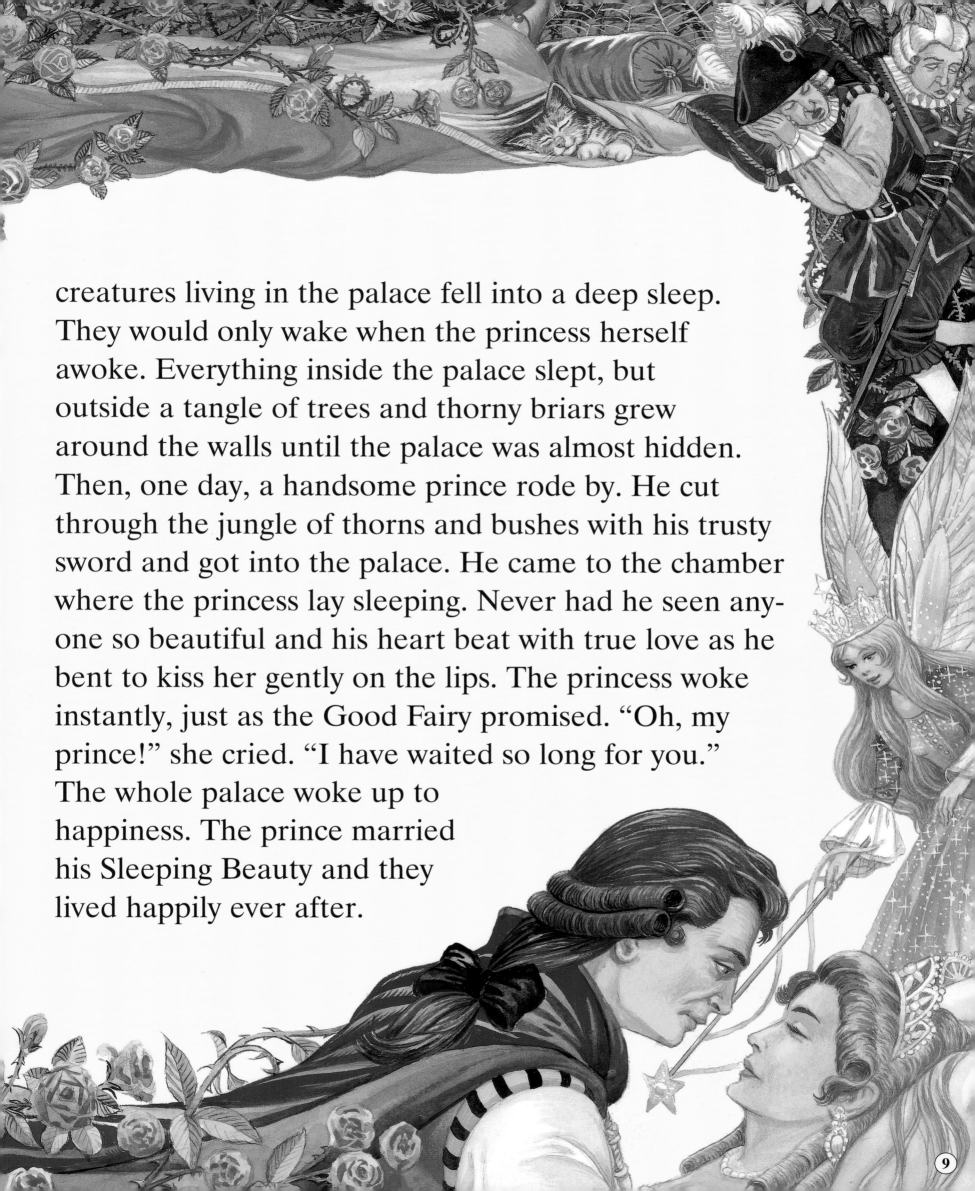

creatures living in the palace fell into a deep sleep. They would only wake when the princess herself awoke. Everything inside the palace slept, but outside a tangle of trees and thorny briars grew around the walls until the palace was almost hidden. Then, one day, a handsome prince rode by. He cut through the jungle of thorns and bushes with his trusty sword and got into the palace. He came to the chamber where the princess lay sleeping. Never had he seen any-one so beautiful and his heart beat with true love as he bent to kiss her gently on the lips. The princess woke instantly, just as the Good Fairy promised. "Oh, my prince!" she cried. "I have waited so long for you." The whole palace woke up to happiness. The prince married his Sleeping Beauty and they lived happily ever after.

The Brave Tin Soldier

The boy took the lid off the box. 'Tin soldiers for my birthday! I'll line them up on the table!' There were twenty five soldiers, each one in a uniform of red and blue. One tin soldier had only one leg, because there had not been enough tin to finish him. But he stood as firmly on his one leg as the other soldiers did on their two legs. The boy had a toy castle with swans swimming on a silver lake and toy trees all around. At the door stood a paper doll. She was a dancer in a pretty dress with a blue ribbon over her shoulders and a big tinsel rose at her neck.

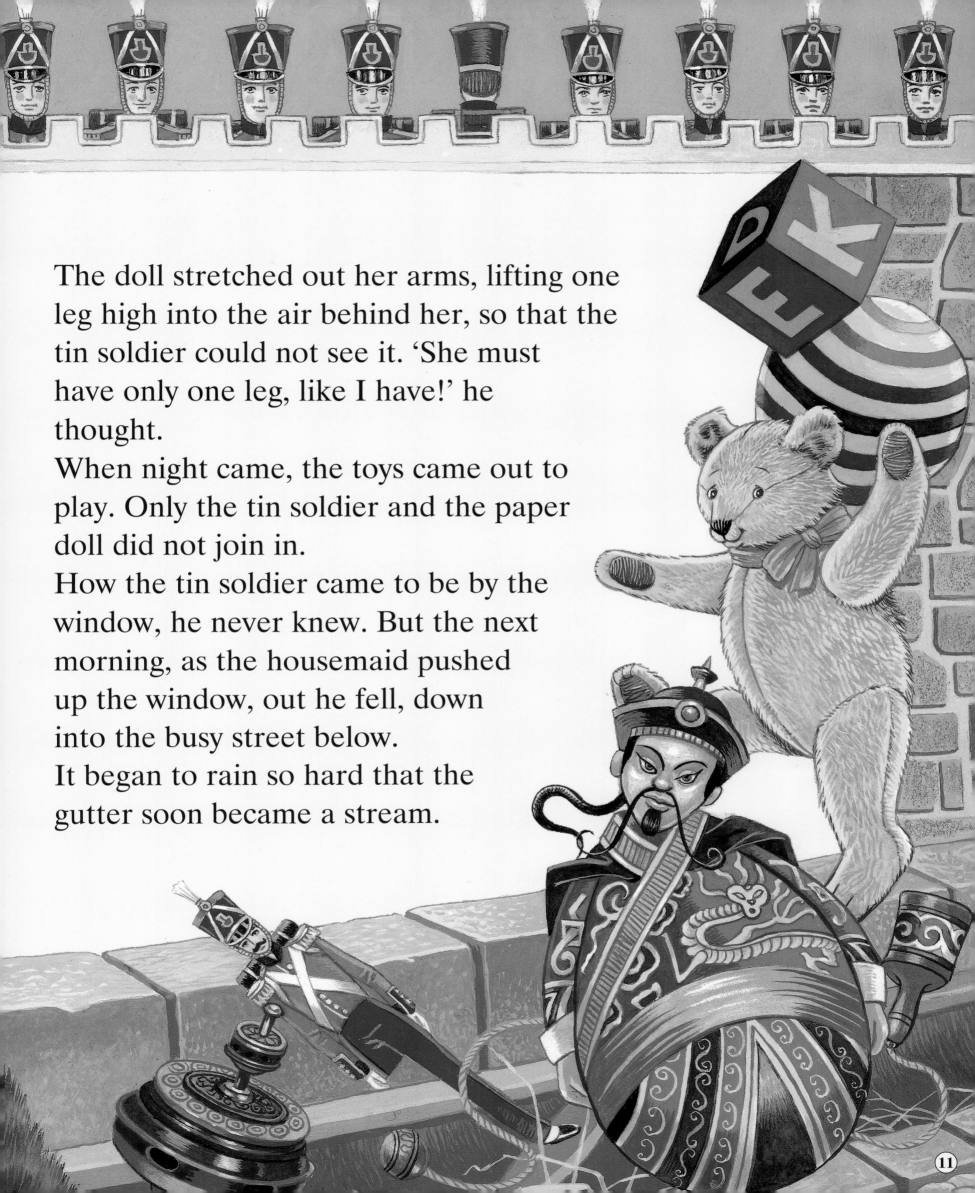

The doll stretched out her arms, lifting one leg high into the air behind her, so that the tin soldier could not see it. 'She must have only one leg, like I have!' he thought.

When night came, the toys came out to play. Only the tin soldier and the paper doll did not join in.

How the tin soldier came to be by the window, he never knew. But the next morning, as the housemaid pushed up the window, out he fell, down into the busy street below.

It began to rain so hard that the gutter soon became a stream.

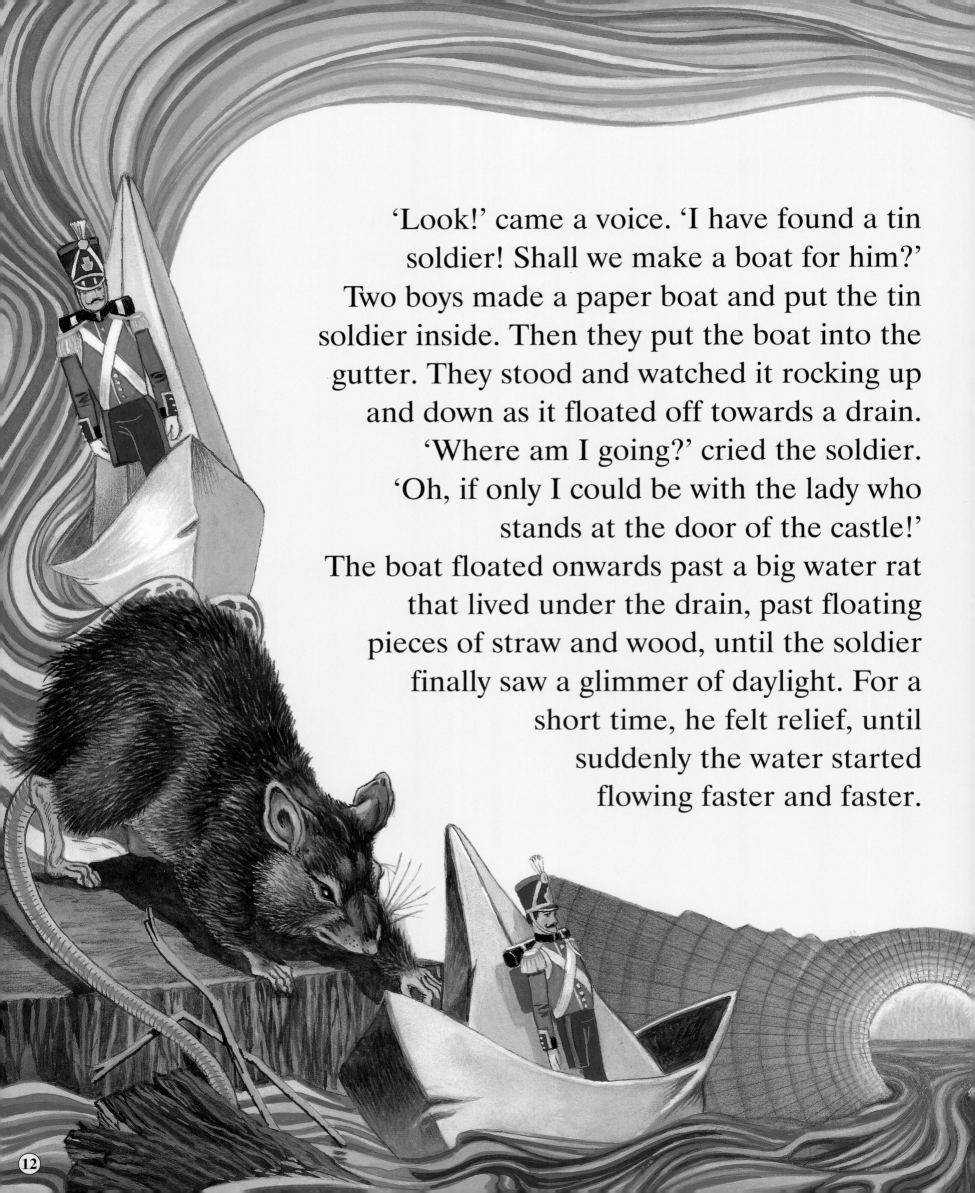

'Look!' came a voice. 'I have found a tin soldier! Shall we make a boat for him?' Two boys made a paper boat and put the tin soldier inside. Then they put the boat into the gutter. They stood and watched it rocking up and down as it floated off towards a drain. 'Where am I going?' cried the soldier. 'Oh, if only I could be with the lady who stands at the door of the castle!' The boat floated onwards past a big water rat that lived under the drain, past floating pieces of straw and wood, until the soldier finally saw a glimmer of daylight. For a short time, he felt relief, until suddenly the water started flowing faster and faster.

The speed of the water made the paper boat whirl round and round until it sank down, taking the tin soldier down with it.

All the tin soldier could think of was the lady at the castle door. Would he ever see her again, he wondered to himself? Suddenly he saw a huge mouth opening in front of him. Then, he was inside the body of a big fish. It was so dark that he could not see anything. Suddenly the tin soldier felt very frightened.

The tin soldier felt the fish swimming to and fro. Then it became quite still. After a short time, something flashed through it, and suddenly he could see daylight.

'Why, it's that tin soldier!' came the voice of the cook. 'He must have been swallowed up by the fish I've just bought at the market!'

She took the soldier to show the family. How happy he was to see the lady at the castle door, standing on one leg and reaching out towards him!

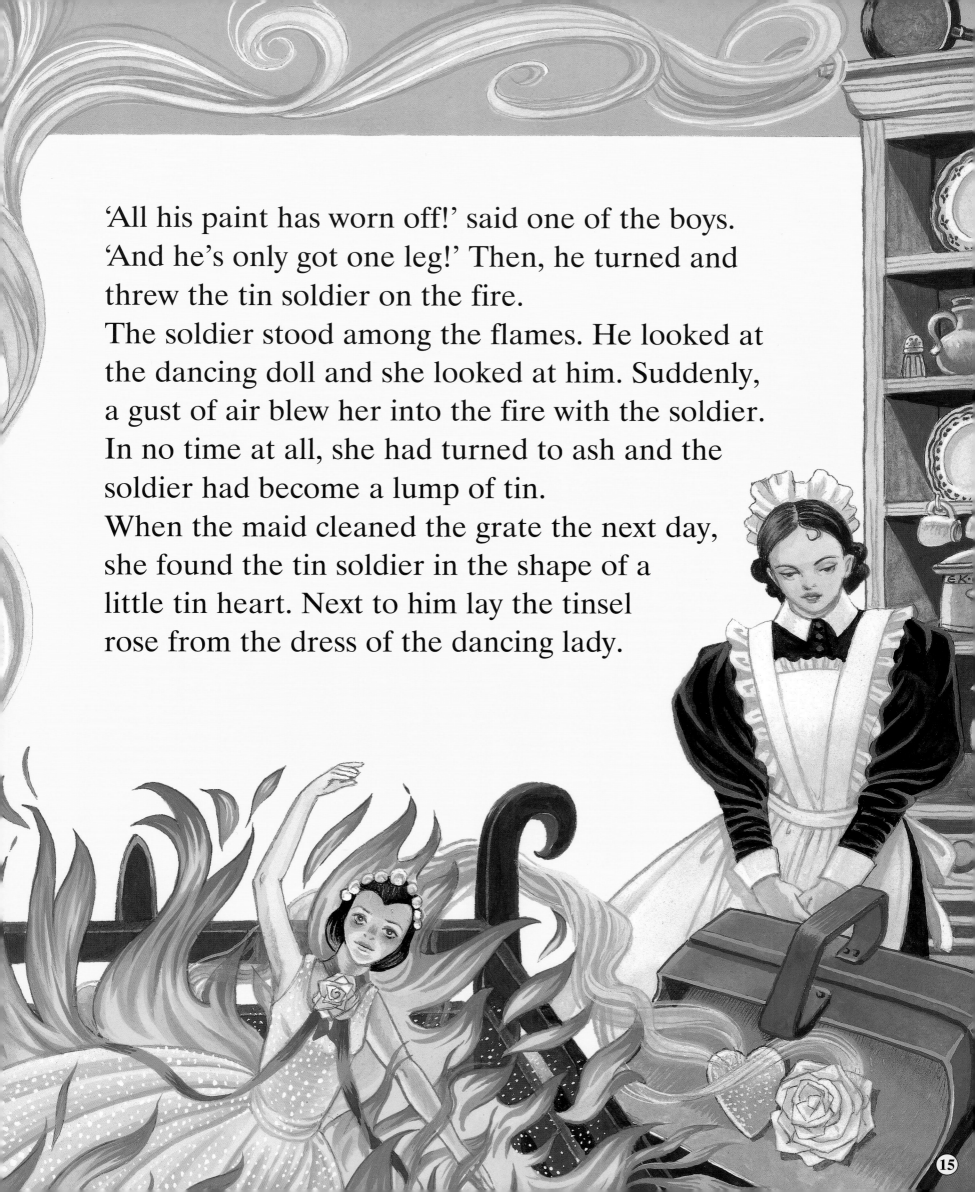

'All his paint has worn off!' said one of the boys. 'And he's only got one leg!' Then, he turned and threw the tin soldier on the fire.

The soldier stood among the flames. He looked at the dancing doll and she looked at him. Suddenly, a gust of air blew her into the fire with the soldier. In no time at all, she had turned to ash and the soldier had become a lump of tin.

When the maid cleaned the grate the next day, she found the tin soldier in the shape of a little tin heart. Next to him lay the tinsel rose from the dress of the dancing lady.

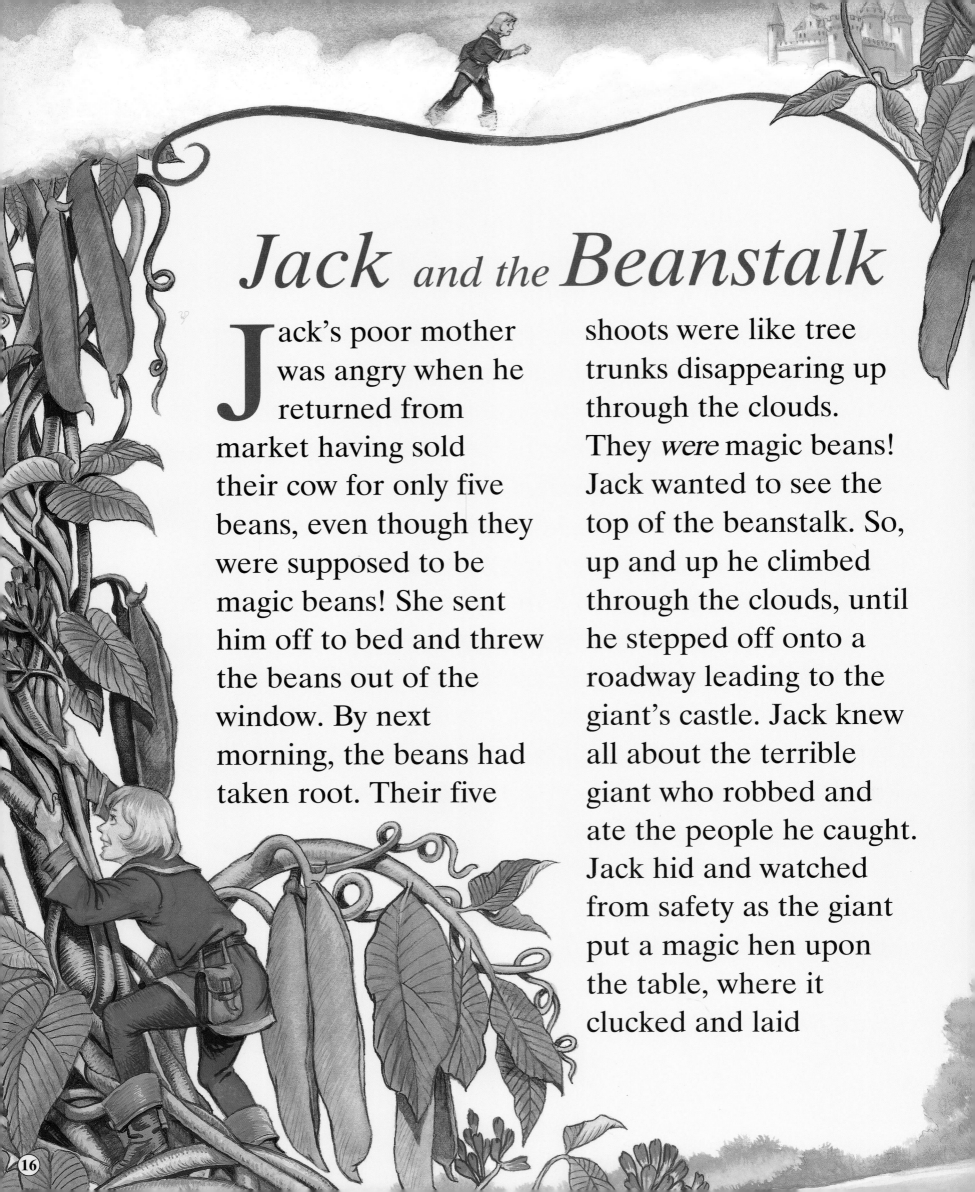

Jack *and the* Beanstalk

Jack's poor mother was angry when he returned from market having sold their cow for only five beans, even though they were supposed to be magic beans! She sent him off to bed and threw the beans out of the window. By next morning, the beans had taken root. Their five shoots were like tree trunks disappearing up through the clouds. They *were* magic beans! Jack wanted to see the top of the beanstalk. So, up and up he climbed through the clouds, until he stepped off onto a roadway leading to the giant's castle. Jack knew all about the terrible giant who robbed and ate the people he caught. Jack hid and watched from safety as the giant put a magic hen upon the table, where it clucked and laid

a golden egg. Jack thought such a hen would be an ideal gift for his mother. So, when the giant settled down to sleep, Jack crept out of hiding and grabbed the hen. The hen squawked and the giant woke up to chase Jack back to the beanstalk. Jack climbed down at top speed, with the puffing giant close behind. On the ground, Jack gave the hen to his astonished mother. He fetched an axe and chopped down the beanstalk. Down came the giant, too.

He hit the ground hard and made a hole so deep that he never got out again. After that, Jack and his mother lived happily on the money they received from selling the golden eggs.

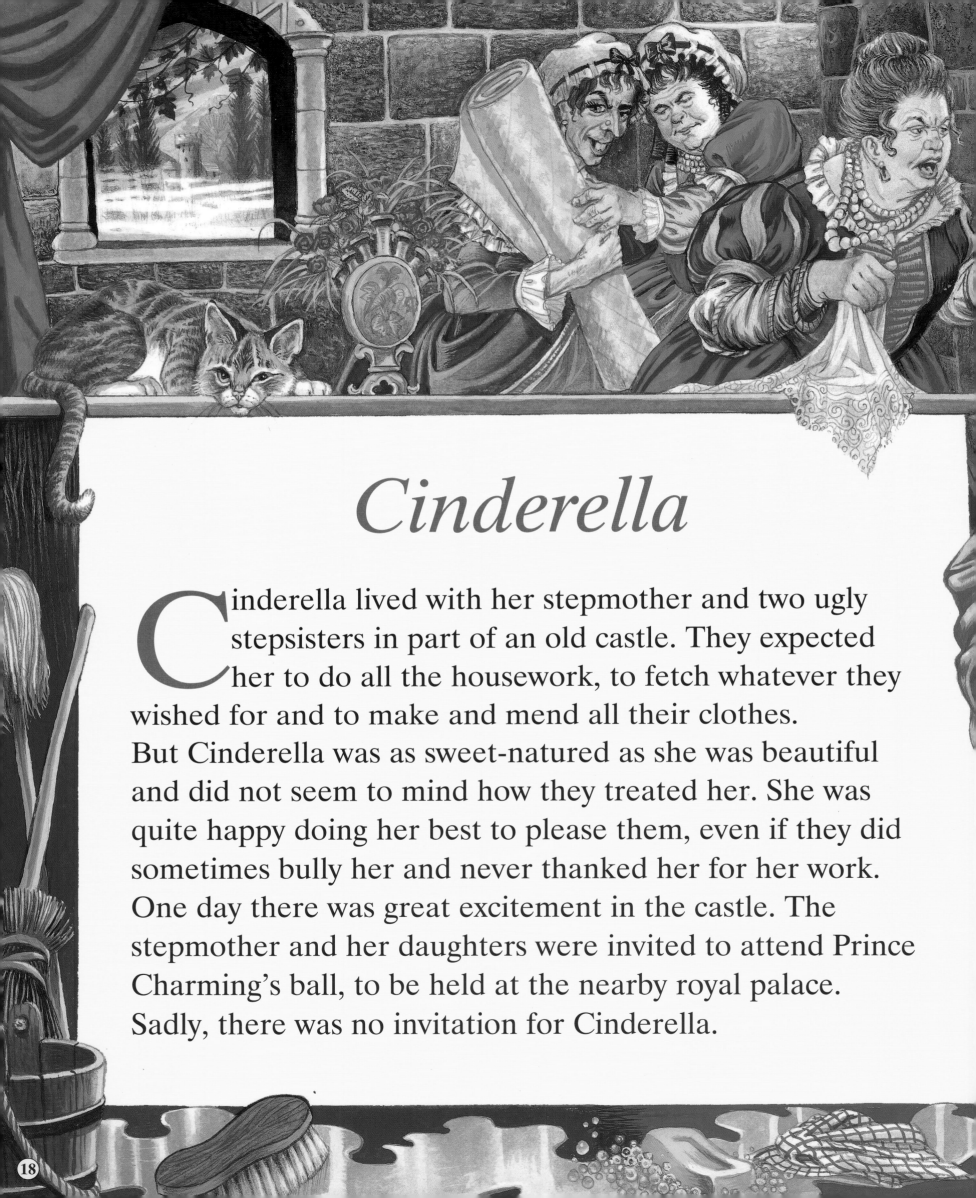

Cinderella

Cinderella lived with her stepmother and two ugly stepsisters in part of an old castle. They expected her to do all the housework, to fetch whatever they wished for and to make and mend all their clothes. But Cinderella was as sweet-natured as she was beautiful and did not seem to mind how they treated her. She was quite happy doing her best to please them, even if they did sometimes bully her and never thanked her for her work. One day there was great excitement in the castle. The stepmother and her daughters were invited to attend Prince Charming's ball, to be held at the nearby royal palace. Sadly, there was no invitation for Cinderella.

"The prince would never invite
Cinderella to the palace ball," laughed
the ugly sisters. "Just look at her ragged clothes!"
The stepmother went out to buy the finest materials with
her daughters, from which Cinderella would have to
make their new ball gowns. That meant more hard work
for Cinderella. She worked from morning until night and
soon the gowns were ready to be fitted. "Don't I look
beautiful?" exclaimed one stepsister. "The prince will
want to dance with me!" boasted her sister.

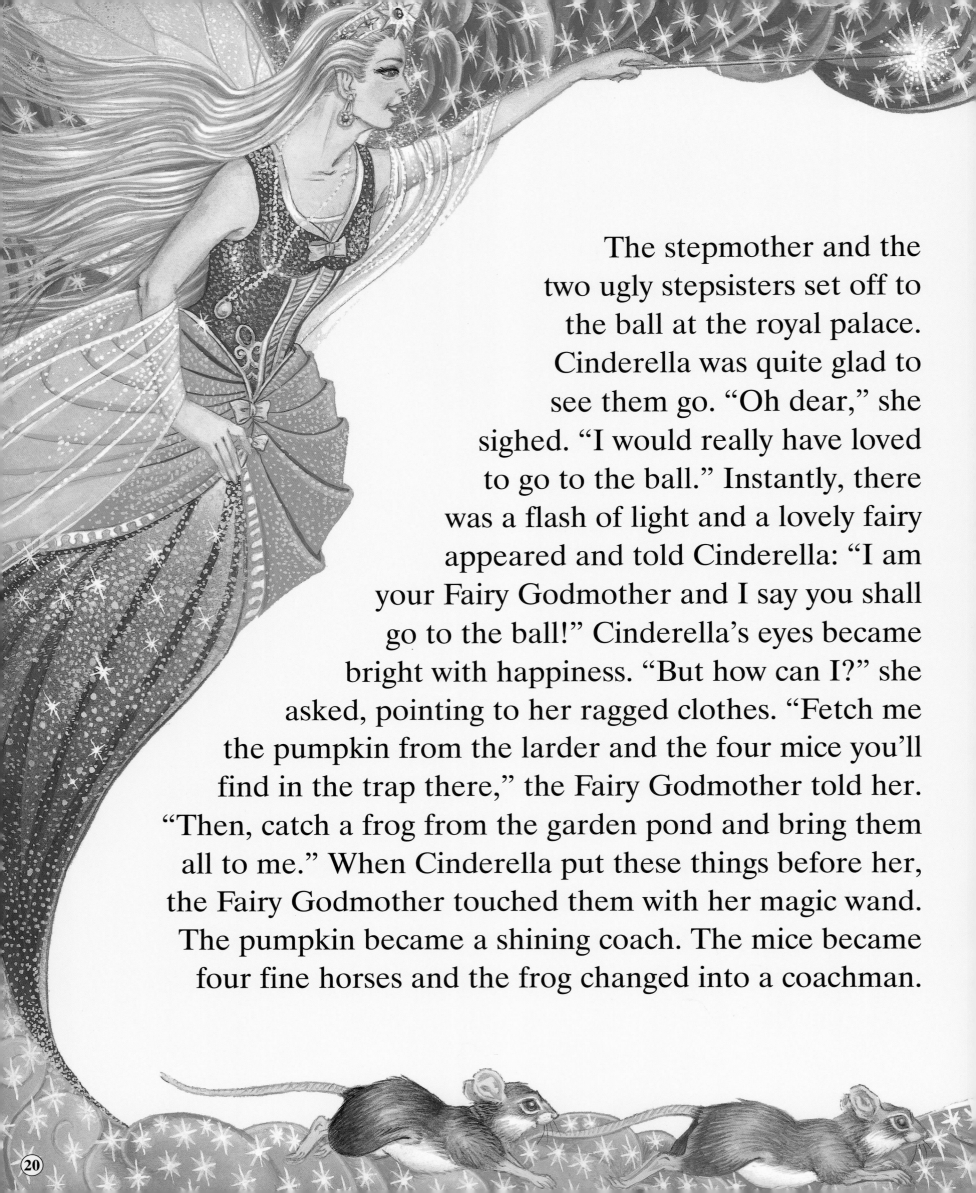

The stepmother and the two ugly stepsisters set off to the ball at the royal palace. Cinderella was quite glad to see them go. "Oh dear," she sighed. "I would really have loved to go to the ball." Instantly, there was a flash of light and a lovely fairy appeared and told Cinderella: "I am your Fairy Godmother and I say you shall go to the ball!" Cinderella's eyes became bright with happiness. "But how can I?" she asked, pointing to her ragged clothes. "Fetch me the pumpkin from the larder and the four mice you'll find in the trap there," the Fairy Godmother told her. "Then, catch a frog from the garden pond and bring them all to me." When Cinderella put these things before her, the Fairy Godmother touched them with her magic wand. The pumpkin became a shining coach. The mice became four fine horses and the frog changed into a coachman.

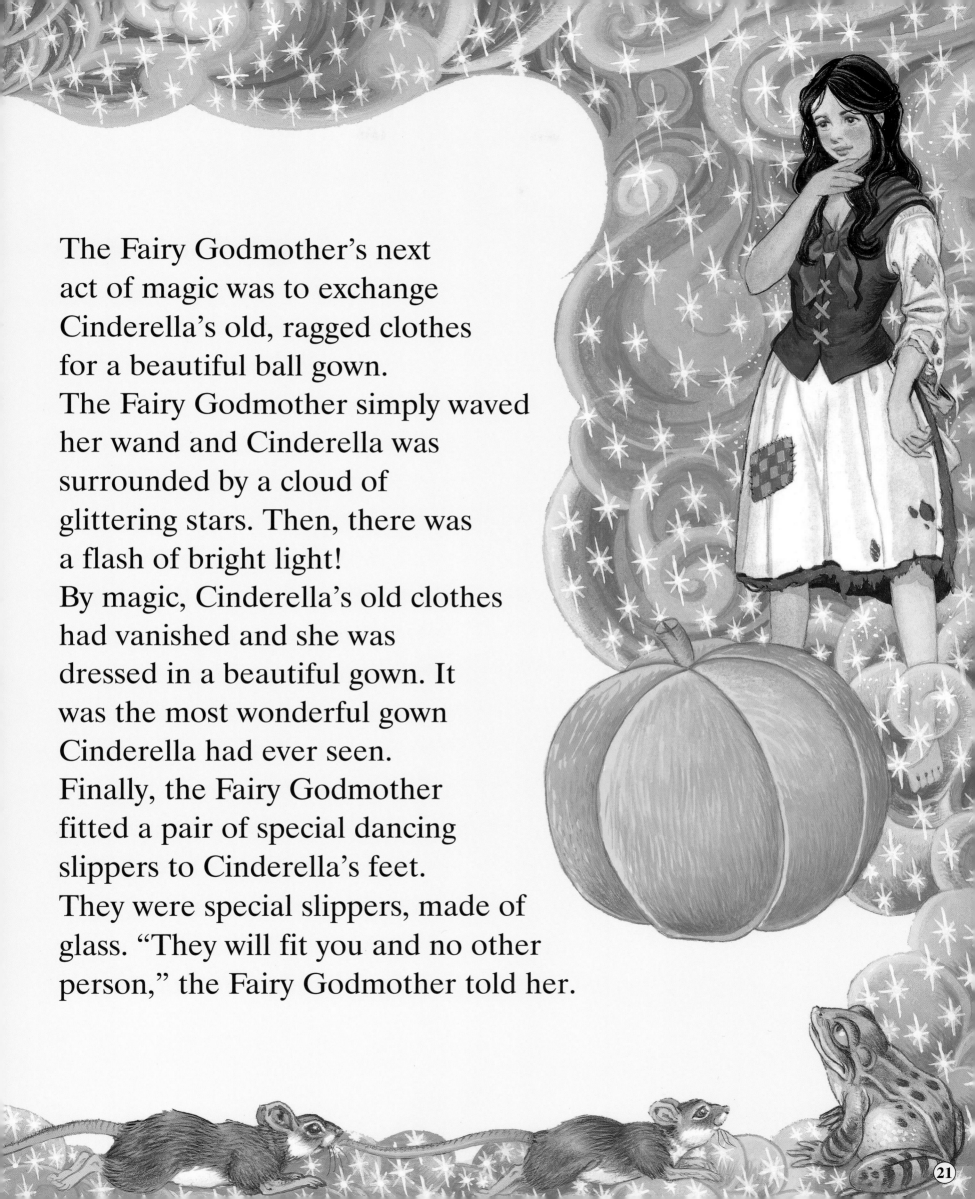

The Fairy Godmother's next
act of magic was to exchange
Cinderella's old, ragged clothes
for a beautiful ball gown.
The Fairy Godmother simply waved
her wand and Cinderella was
surrounded by a cloud of
glittering stars. Then, there was
a flash of bright light!
By magic, Cinderella's old clothes
had vanished and she was
dressed in a beautiful gown. It
was the most wonderful gown
Cinderella had ever seen.
Finally, the Fairy Godmother
fitted a pair of special dancing
slippers to Cinderella's feet.
They were special slippers, made of
glass. "They will fit you and no other
person," the Fairy Godmother told her.

Then the Fairy Godmother warned Cinderella she must leave the ball before midnight. "As the clock strikes," she told Cinderella, "my magic will run out. Your fine clothes will vanish and you'll be dressed in rags again." Cinderella promised to remember and she climbed into her coach and headed for the bright lights of the palace. Everyone at the ball was so enchanted by her beauty that she wasn't asked to show an invitation card. Not even her stepmother or stepsisters recognised her. As for Prince Charming, he fell instantly in love with the beautiful girl he'd never seen before and danced with no other partner. Cinderella was so enjoying herself, she forgot the time. Then, as the clock began to strike midnight, she fled from the ball and one of her glass slippers came off as she ran down the palace steps.

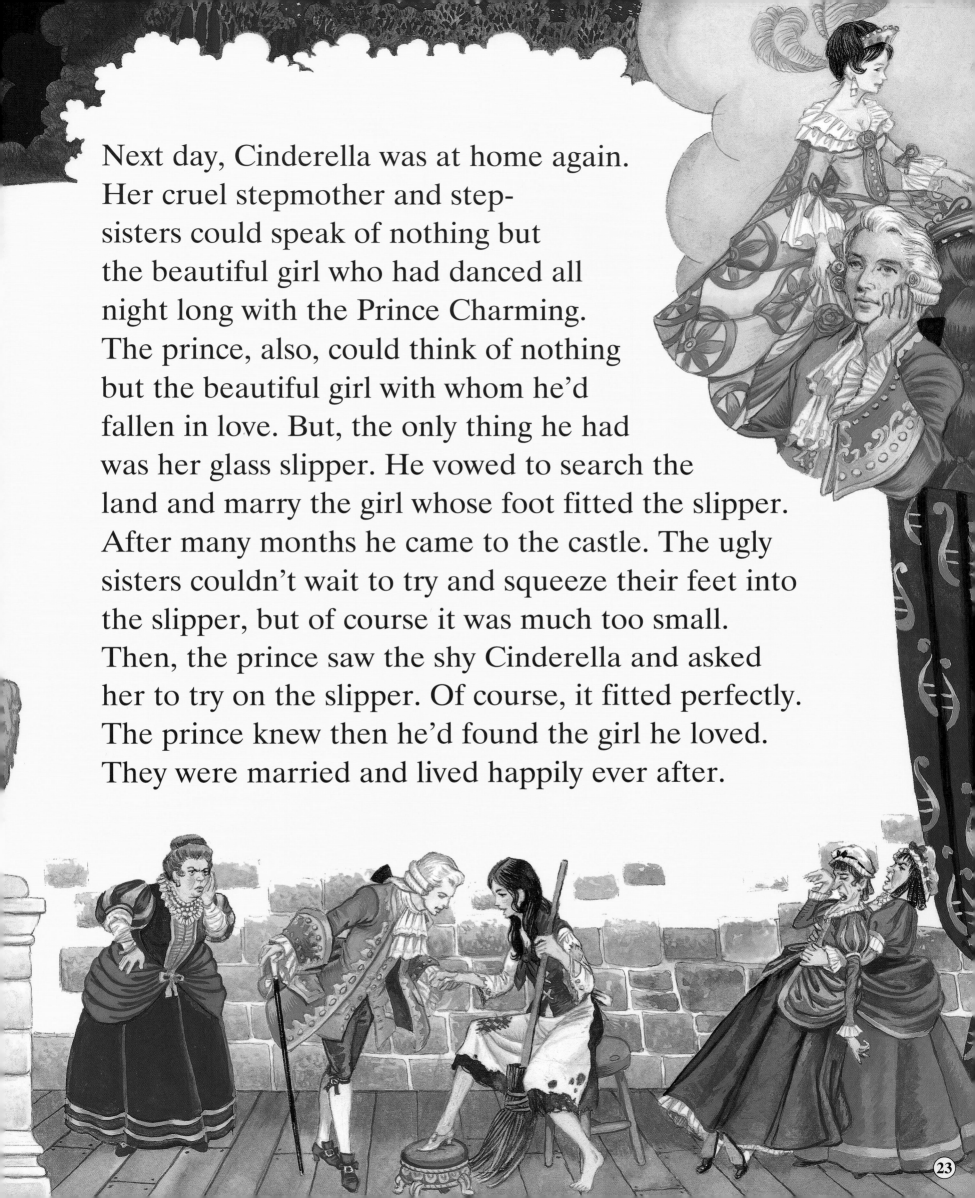

Next day, Cinderella was at home again.
Her cruel stepmother and stepsisters could speak of nothing but
the beautiful girl who had danced all
night long with the Prince Charming.
The prince, also, could think of nothing
but the beautiful girl with whom he'd
fallen in love. But, the only thing he had
was her glass slipper. He vowed to search the
land and marry the girl whose foot fitted the slipper.
After many months he came to the castle. The ugly
sisters couldn't wait to try and squeeze their feet into
the slipper, but of course it was much too small.
Then, the prince saw the shy Cinderella and asked
her to try on the slipper. Of course, it fitted perfectly.
The prince knew then he'd found the girl he loved.
They were married and lived happily ever after.

Thumbelina

There was once a lady who had always wanted a child. 'Plant this seed in a flower pot!' said a kindly old witch. 'See what happens!' Well, that seed grew into such a beautiful tulip that the lady kissed it. The leaves opened and there sat a lovely little girl, only half as high as her thumb. 'Oh!' she cried. 'I will call you Thumbelina!' Half a walnut shell became a little cradle for Thumbelina, with a rose leaf to keep her warm. By day, she rowed a tulip leaf across a pond, using two hairs for oars.

Then one night, a toad hopped in and took the walnut shell with Thumbelina inside it. The next thing she knew, she was on a water-lily!
'See how beautiful she is, my son!' came the toad's voice. 'She will make you a fine wife!' Thumbelina covered her tiny face and wept. She did not want to marry an ugly toad! The fish felt sorry for her, so they worked together, nibbling the stalk of the water-lily until it broke free.

Then, Thumbelina stood on the water-lily as it floated along, pulled by a butterfly. How lovely it was to be far away from the ugly toad!

She did not see a big beetle flying towards her, until he had picked her up and flown into a large tree!

'She only has two legs!' said one beetle.

'And NO feelers!' said a second.

'She looks HUMAN!' added a third. 'How ugly!' 'You are right,' said the first beetle. 'We shall leave her in the wood.'

Now, Thumbelina was quite alone. She made a hammock from grass, with a nettle for shelter. She ate honey from the flowers and drank dew from the leaves. Then came the winter. The birds flew away. Leaves withered and snow began to fall. The smell of corn that a field-mouse had stocked up for the winter made her feel so hungry.

'Please,' begged Thumbelina, 'will you give me something to eat?' 'Poor creature!' said the mouse. 'Come in!' So, Thumbelina stayed with the mouse. He looked after her and told her stories. 'Mole has dug a tunnel, so we can visit!' said the mouse. 'He says we should not be afraid of the dead bird in the tunnel.' But when Thumbelina saw the beautiful swallow, she felt very sad. That night, she made a blanket of hay to put over the bird. But the swallow was not dead, only stiff with the cold. Soon, the swallow opened her eyes and for the rest of the winter, Thumbelina looked after her. 'Sit on my back, Thumbelina!' said the swallow. 'We shall fly away!' 'I cannot leave the field-mouse!' said Thumbelina. 'He has been so kind to me!' She was sad to see the swallow go. But the mouse was too excited to notice.

'Thumbelina!' he said. 'Mole wants to marry you! You will not see so much of the sun once you are his wife and living under the earth!'

Thumbelina hated the idea of marrying Mole! 'Farewell, sun!' she said. 'Say hello to the swallow for me!'

'Tweet-tweet!' It seemed Thumbelina was dreaming. Then the sound came again. 'Tweet-tweet!'

'My own little swallow!' cried Thumbelina. 'Come with me to a warmer land!' said the swallow. So Thumbelina climbed on the bird's back and the swallow flew over forests and lakes and high mountains, until they came to the warmer countries. Here, the sun shone and the air was sweet with the smell of fruit and flowers. Far below, Thumbelina saw a palace of white marble with tall pillars.

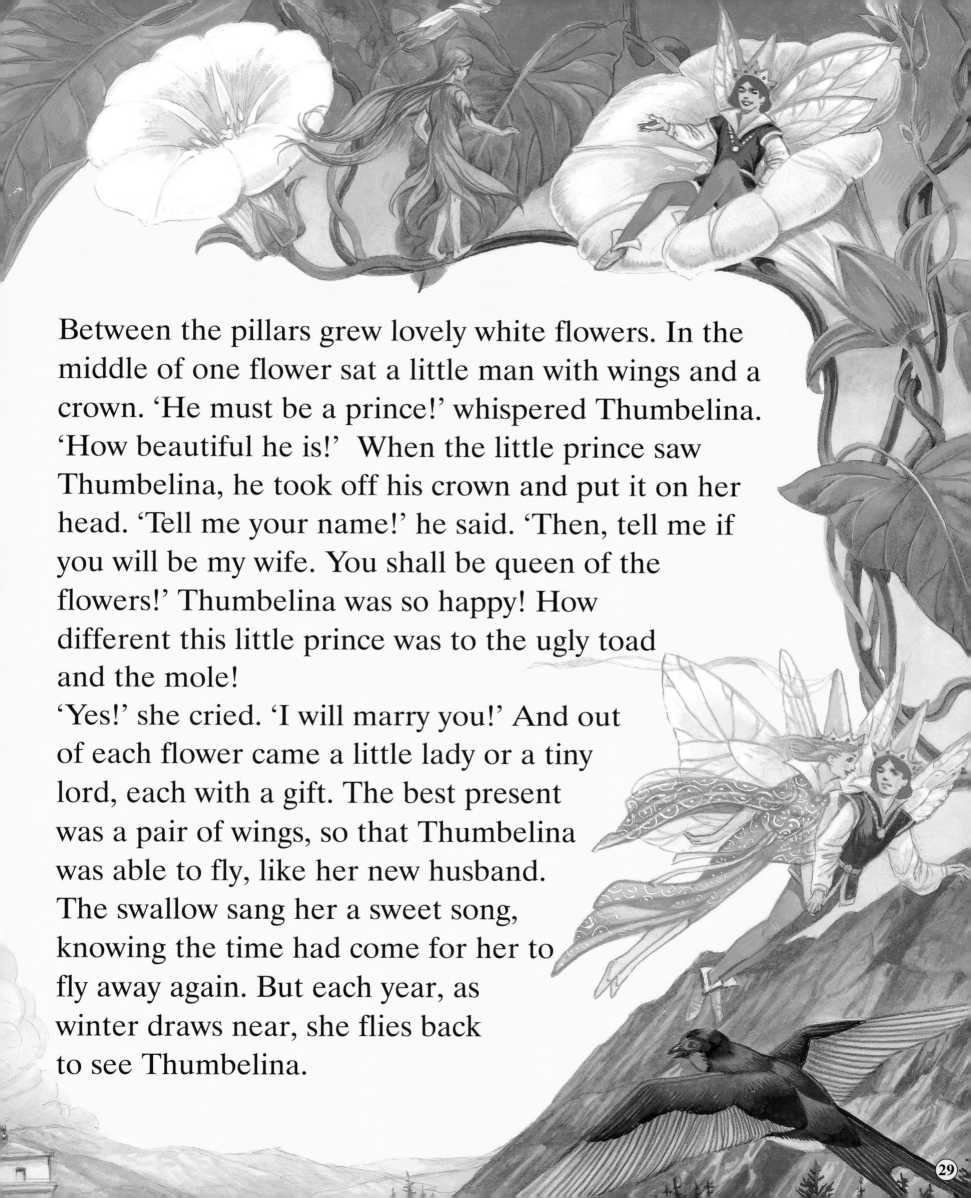

Between the pillars grew lovely white flowers. In the middle of one flower sat a little man with wings and a crown. 'He must be a prince!' whispered Thumbelina. 'How beautiful he is!' When the little prince saw Thumbelina, he took off his crown and put it on her head. 'Tell me your name!' he said. 'Then, tell me if you will be my wife. You shall be queen of the flowers!' Thumbelina was so happy! How different this little prince was to the ugly toad and the mole!

'Yes!' she cried. 'I will marry you!' And out of each flower came a little lady or a tiny lord, each with a gift. The best present was a pair of wings, so that Thumbelina was able to fly, like her new husband. The swallow sang her a sweet song, knowing the time had come for her to fly away again. But each year, as winter draws near, she flies back to see Thumbelina.

Red Riding Hood

Once each week, Red Riding Hood walked through the forest to take a basket of food to her dear old grandmother.

The hungry wolf licked his lips when he saw her. He did not attack her, as he knew the wood-cutter, working nearby, would come to the rescue of little Red Riding Hood.

The wolf thought he had a better idea. He would run on ahead to her grandmother's cottage, frighten her away and then lie there waiting for little Red Riding Hood to arrive. Grandmother ran away screaming at the sight of the wolf. The wolf quickly dressed up in her long nightgown and her sleeping cap.

He leapt into bed waiting for Red Riding Hood to arrive.

"Come in, my dear!" said the wolf in a squeaky voice, when Red Riding Hood knocked on the door.

"What a funny voice you have got, Grandma!" said Red Riding Hood. "And your ears have grown really big!"

"All the better to hear you with, my dear," said the wolf. "And what big teeth you have!" said Red Riding Hood.

"All the better to eat you with, my dear!" roared the wolf as he leapt up to try and grab Red Riding Hood.

"Help! Help!" cried little Red Riding Hood. She ran from the cottage into the arms of her grandmother, who had called for the wood-cutter. He scared the wolf so it ran off and was never seen again!

The Little

Far out to sea, in a castle of coral and shells lived the Sea King with his mother and six daughters. All six mermaids were pretty, but the youngest was the most beautiful. Her one treasure was a statue of a young man. She had rescued it from a sunken ship and put it in her underwater garden.

One by one, her sisters went up out of the sea and into the world beyond. 'Soon it will be time for you to rise up out of the sea, too!' said her grandmother.

At last came the day for the little mermaid to swim up to the surface of the sea. She raised her head above the water to see a ship lit with lanterns. She swam closer to hear the music, with people celebrating the birthday of their prince. Fireworks rose into the sky, lighting up the ship. The little mermaid was frightened. Then she saw the prince. 'How handsome he is!' she thought. 'Just like my statue!'

Mermaid

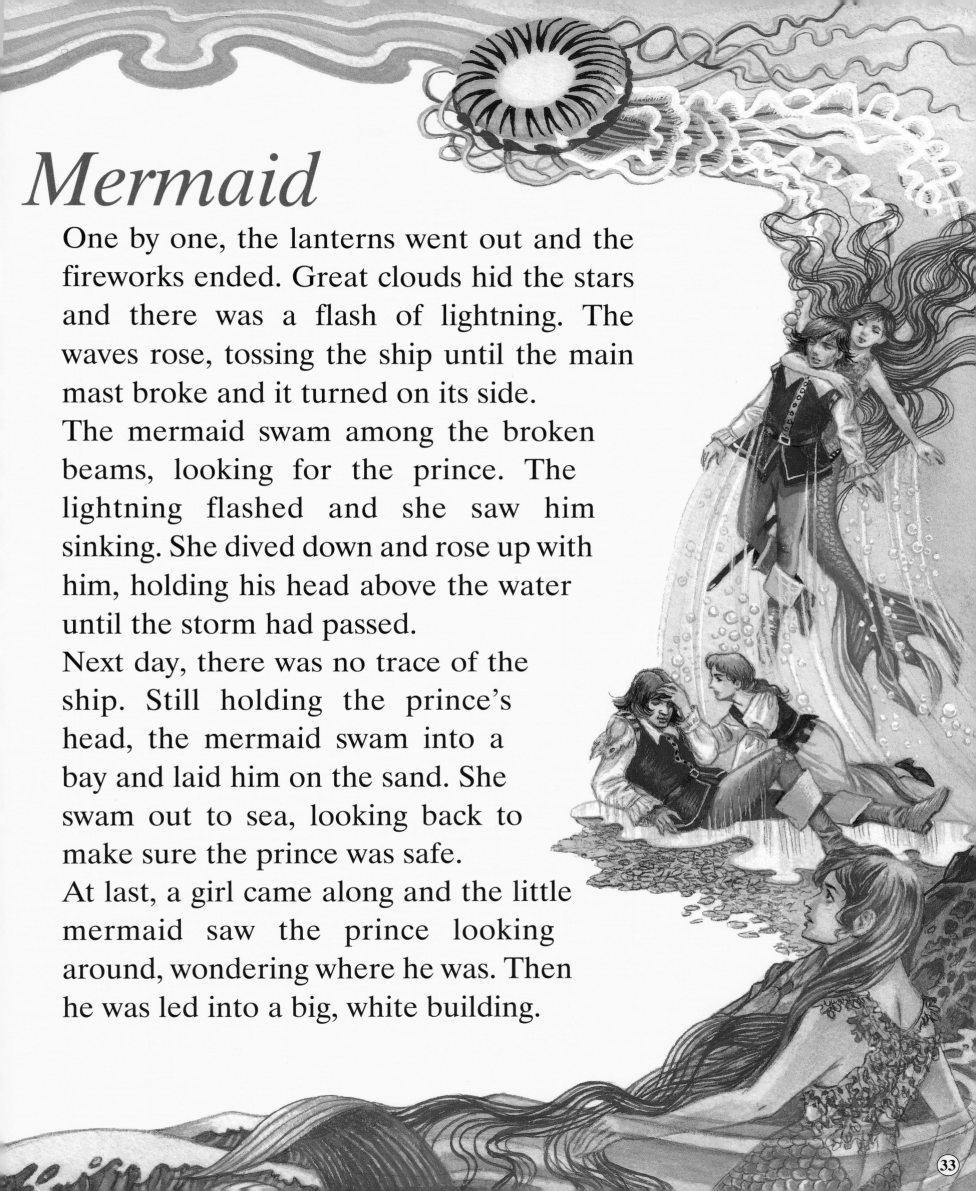

One by one, the lanterns went out and the fireworks ended. Great clouds hid the stars and there was a flash of lightning. The waves rose, tossing the ship until the main mast broke and it turned on its side.

The mermaid swam among the broken beams, looking for the prince. The lightning flashed and she saw him sinking. She dived down and rose up with him, holding his head above the water until the storm had passed.

Next day, there was no trace of the ship. Still holding the prince's head, the mermaid swam into a bay and laid him on the sand. She swam out to sea, looking back to make sure the prince was safe.

At last, a girl came along and the little mermaid saw the prince looking around, wondering where he was. Then he was led into a big, white building.

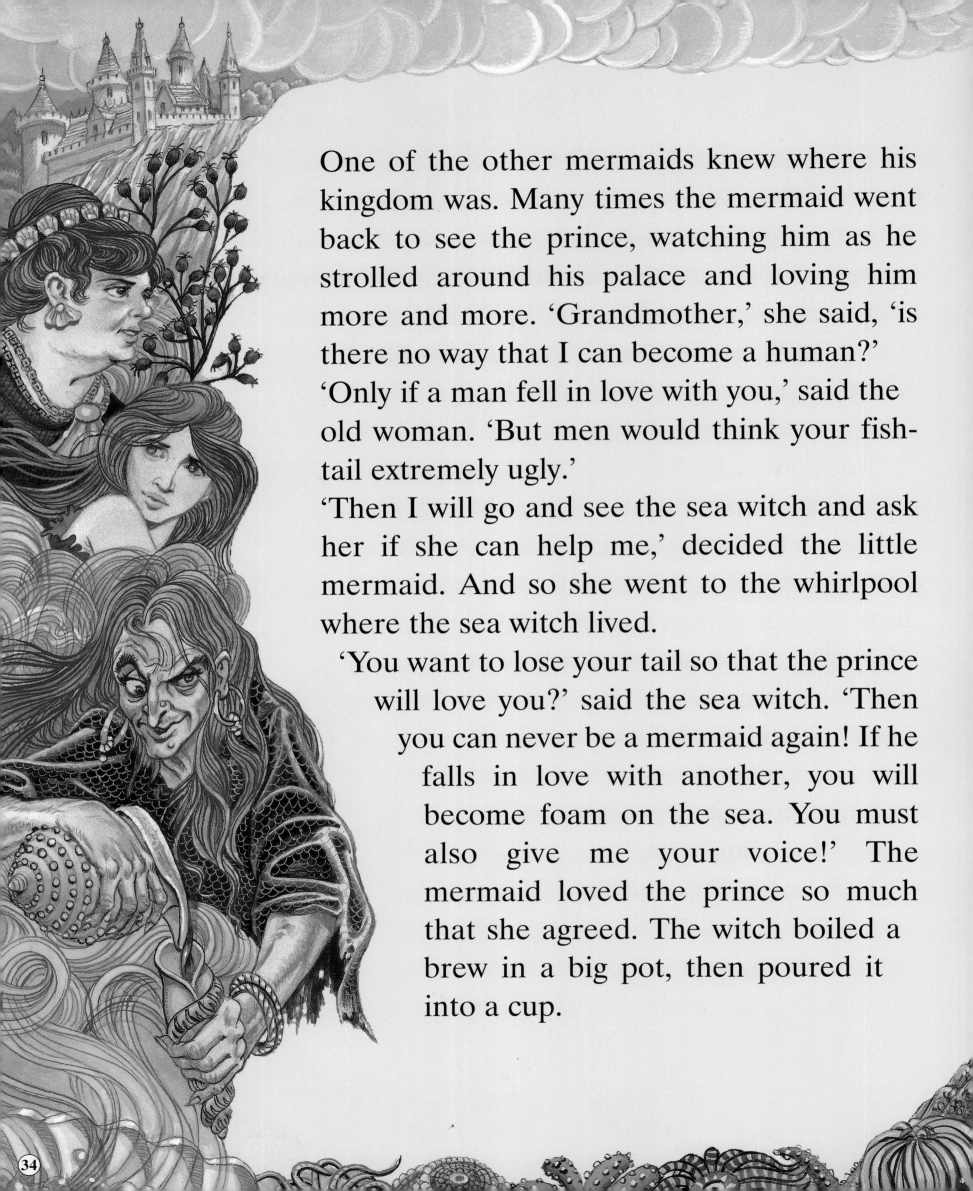

One of the other mermaids knew where his kingdom was. Many times the mermaid went back to see the prince, watching him as he strolled around his palace and loving him more and more. 'Grandmother,' she said, 'is there no way that I can become a human?'

'Only if a man fell in love with you,' said the old woman. 'But men would think your fish-tail extremely ugly.'

'Then I will go and see the sea witch and ask her if she can help me,' decided the little mermaid. And so she went to the whirlpool where the sea witch lived.

'You want to lose your tail so that the prince will love you?' said the sea witch. 'Then you can never be a mermaid again! If he falls in love with another, you will become foam on the sea. You must also give me your voice!' The mermaid loved the prince so much that she agreed. The witch boiled a brew in a big pot, then poured it into a cup.

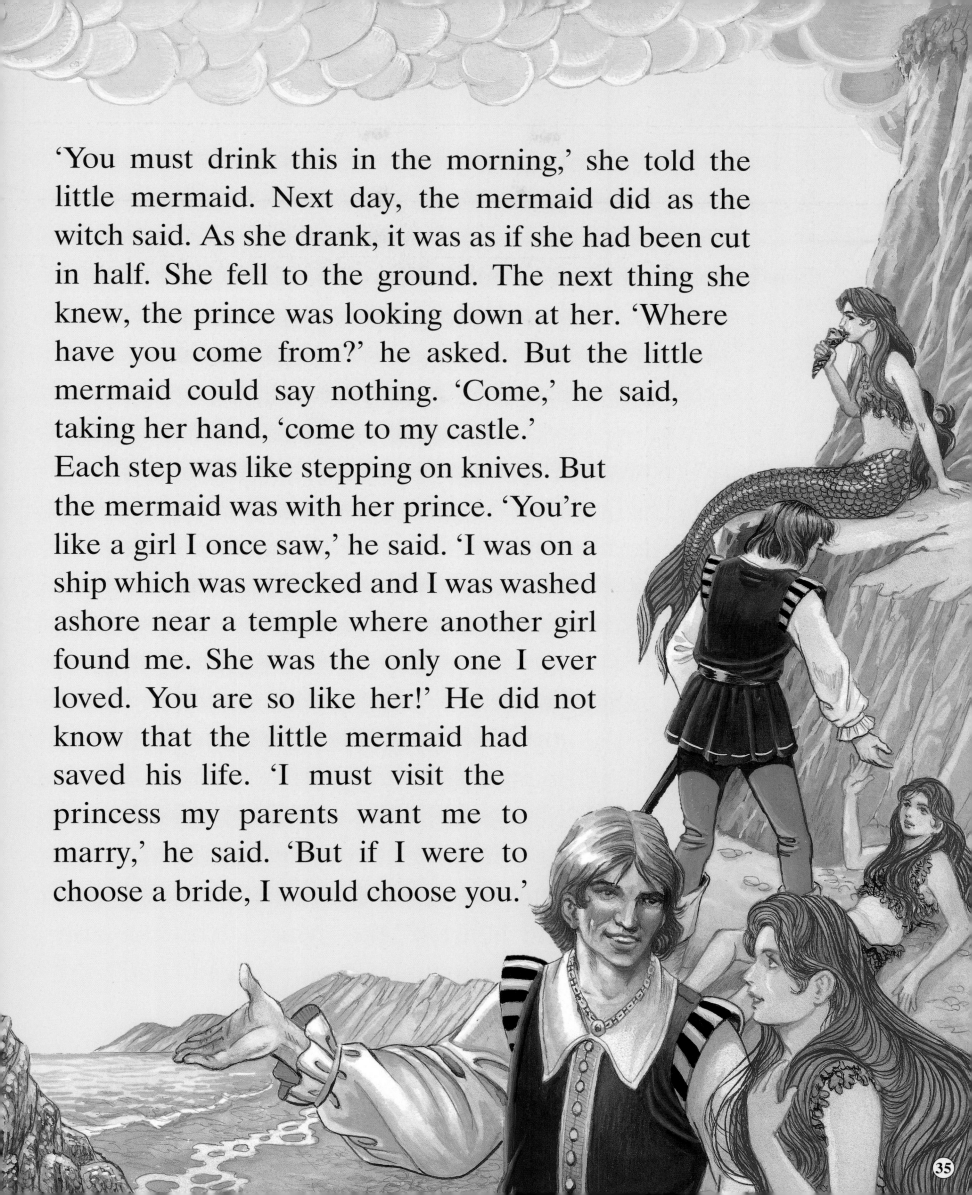

'You must drink this in the morning,' she told the little mermaid. Next day, the mermaid did as the witch said. As she drank, it was as if she had been cut in half. She fell to the ground. The next thing she knew, the prince was looking down at her. 'Where have you come from?' he asked. But the little mermaid could say nothing. 'Come,' he said, taking her hand, 'come to my castle.'

Each step was like stepping on knives. But the mermaid was with her prince. 'You're like a girl I once saw,' he said. 'I was on a ship which was wrecked and I was washed ashore near a temple where another girl found me. She was the only one I ever loved. You are so like her!' He did not know that the little mermaid had saved his life. 'I must visit the princess my parents want me to marry,' he said. 'But if I were to choose a bride, I would choose you.'

The mermaid and the prince sailed to meet the princess. Bells rang and trumpets sounded to welcome the prince as the ship sailed into harbour. Then the princess arrived. 'It was you who saved me when I lay on the shore!' cried the prince.

'I know you will be happy for me,' he said to the little mermaid. She kissed his hand. But her heart was broken. On the day of the wedding, she held the train of the bride's dress, but she hardly heard the wedding music.

That evening, the bride and bridegroom went on board ship. The little mermaid remembered the first time she had seen the prince. Then, as she gazed out to sea, she saw her sisters rising out of the water. Their long hair had all been cut off.

'We gave it to the sea witch so that she would help you!' they cried. 'Before the sun rises, you must thrust this knife into the heart of the prince! It is the only way you will get your fish-tail back and become a mermaid again. Hurry!'

The little mermaid took the knife and crept towards the bed where the prince slept. But she could not bring herself to harm him. Instead, she flung the knife into the sea. Then with one last glance at the prince, she plunged into the water, vanishing into the foam.

Now the sun rose, its beams warming the face of the little mermaid. Thousands of beautiful little beings wavered above her head, drawing the little mermaid up towards them.

Far below, the little mermaid could see the white sails of the prince's ship, the sun and the bright red clouds above her, in the sky. And all the time, the beautiful creatures sang their sweet song, lifting her higher and higher. 'Where are you taking me?' she cried. 'Who are you?' 'We are the daughters of the air!' came the answer. 'We fly to hot countries and bring coolness. We spread the scent of the flowers and bring refreshment. By your good works and your kindness you have raised yourself to our world!' The little mermaid stretched out her arms towards the sun. But there were tears in her eyes.

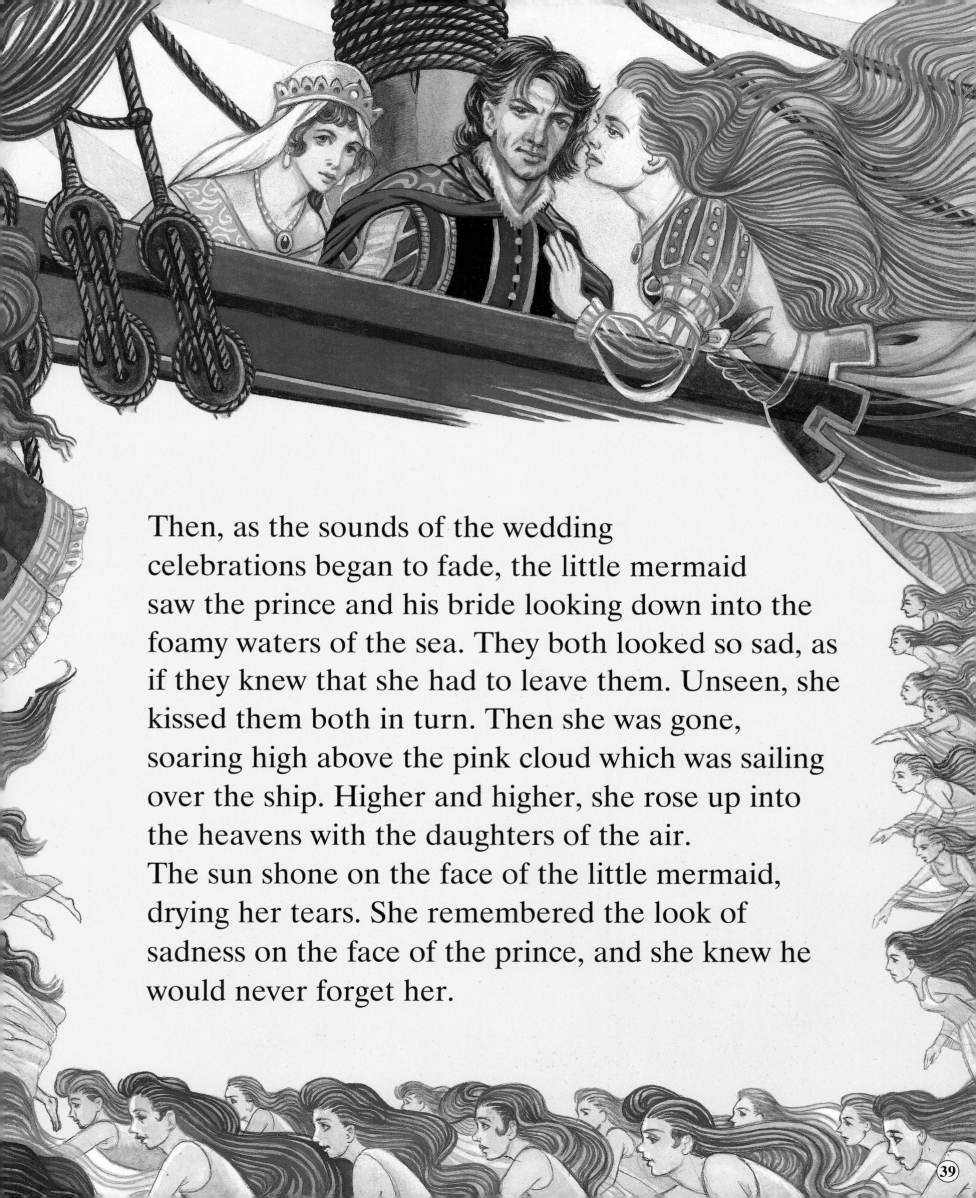

Then, as the sounds of the wedding celebrations began to fade, the little mermaid saw the prince and his bride looking down into the foamy waters of the sea. They both looked so sad, as if they knew that she had to leave them. Unseen, she kissed them both in turn. Then she was gone, soaring high above the pink cloud which was sailing over the ship. Higher and higher, she rose up into the heavens with the daughters of the air.

The sun shone on the face of the little mermaid, drying her tears. She remembered the look of sadness on the face of the prince, and she knew he would never forget her.

Rapunzel

Long ago, a young prince set out to explore beyond his father's kingdom.

One day he found a witch calling up to a window at the top of a tall tower:

"Rapunzel, Rapunzel,
Let down your hair,
So I can climb
The golden stair."

A beautiful girl appeared.

She loosened her long golden hair until its ends reached the ground and the witch climbed up it to join her. When the witch left the tower, the prince came out of hiding and called up to the window:

"Rapunzel, Rapunzel,
Let down your hair,
So I can climb
The golden stair."

The girl appeared and let down her golden hair and the prince climbed up it to join her.

The girl's name was Rapunzel. She was a prisoner of the witch, who wanted the girl as her slave.

But Rapunzel instantly fell in love with the prince. The witch was furious that Rapunzel and the prince had met. In a rage, the witch cut off Rapunzel's hair and banished her to live in a desert. Then, she held Rapunzel's hair from the window so the prince could climb down from the tower. But, she let go and he fell into a bush.

The thorns pierced his eyes. He became blind and wandered into the desert where Rapunzel now lived. By chance, Rapunzel found the blind prince. She held him close and as her tears of love fell upon his face, they healed his eyes and he could see again.

They were able to find their way back to his father's kingdom and lived happily ever after.

Snow White

In a land far away, there once lived a Queen who was very proud of her great beauty. Secretly, she was a wicked witch, able to cast spells and perform all sorts of magic. The Queen had a magic mirror and every day she would look at her reflection in it and ask the question:

"Mirror, mirror on the wall,
Who is the fairest of us all?"

The mirror would always reply:

"You are the fairest of all!"

This pleased the Queen, but she feared the day

when the mirror might give her a different answer. Her stepdaughter, Snow White, was growing up fast and becoming more beautiful each day. Very soon, the day did come when the mirror answered the Queen's question by saying:

"You were the fairest until now –

Now Snow White is fairer yet than thou!"

When the Queen heard these words, she flew into a terrible rage and sent for Black Boris, an evil man who was her Chief Huntsman.

"Boris!" the Queen told her Huntsman. "You will take Princess Snow White deep into the forest and there you will kill her!" Now even the cruel Boris was alarmed by the Queen's terrible order.

"Kill the Princess Snow White?" he moaned.

"Yes, kill her," repeated the Queen, "and then again I shall be the fairest one of all."

Snow White was delighted when Boris invited her to spend a day exploring the forest and she happily climbed up onto his horse. Boris answered all Snow White's many questions about the animals and flowers they saw along the way. Then, deep in the forest, Snow White saw some wild violets. "I must take some home," she said. Snow White jumped down from Boris's horse. Soon she became very busy gathering flowers. She didn't notice he was quietly leading his horse away

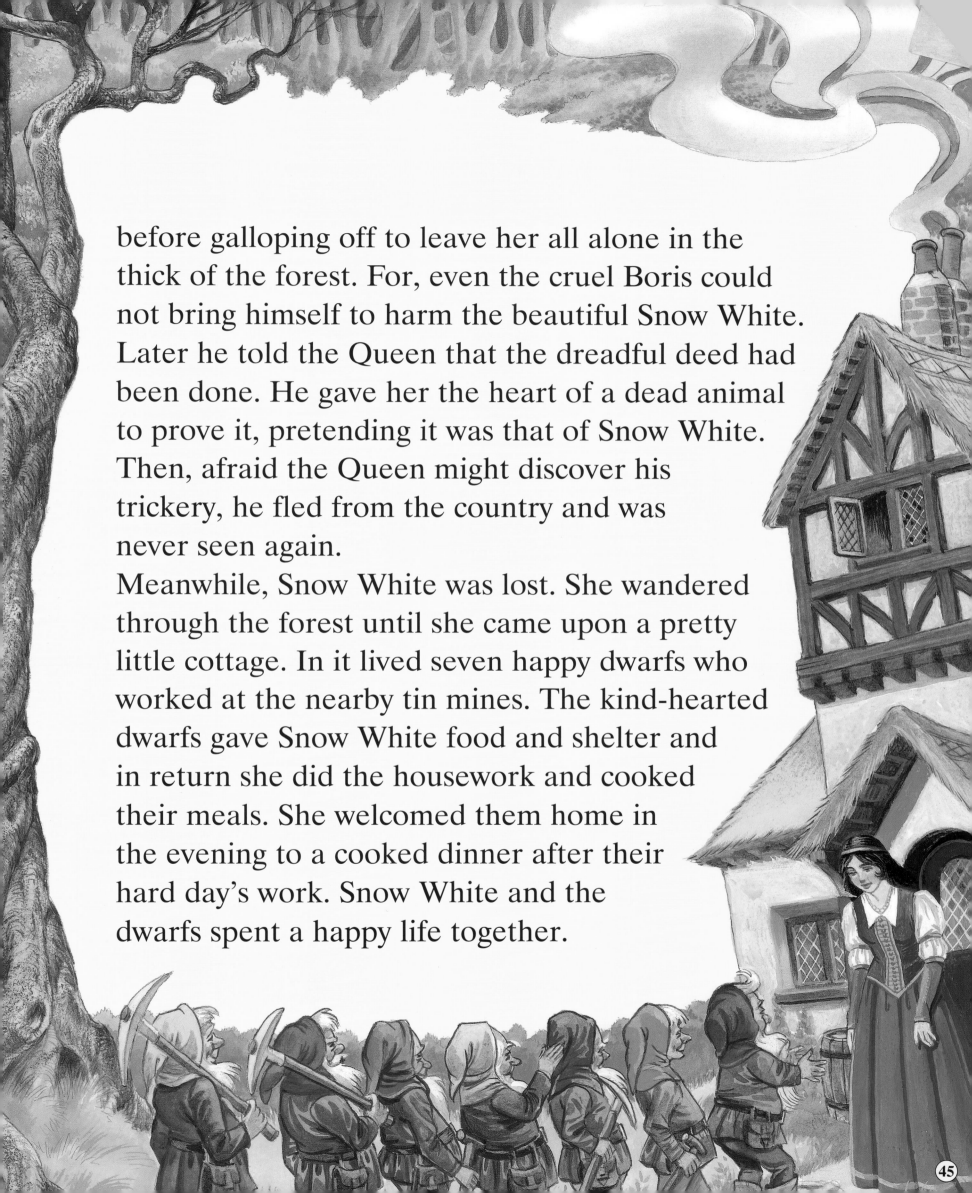

before galloping off to leave her all alone in the thick of the forest. For, even the cruel Boris could not bring himself to harm the beautiful Snow White. Later he told the Queen that the dreadful deed had been done. He gave her the heart of a dead animal to prove it, pretending it was that of Snow White. Then, afraid the Queen might discover his trickery, he fled from the country and was never seen again.

Meanwhile, Snow White was lost. She wandered through the forest until she came upon a pretty little cottage. In it lived seven happy dwarfs who worked at the nearby tin mines. The kind-hearted dwarfs gave Snow White food and shelter and in return she did the housework and cooked their meals. She welcomed them home in the evening to a cooked dinner after their hard day's work. Snow White and the dwarfs spent a happy life together.

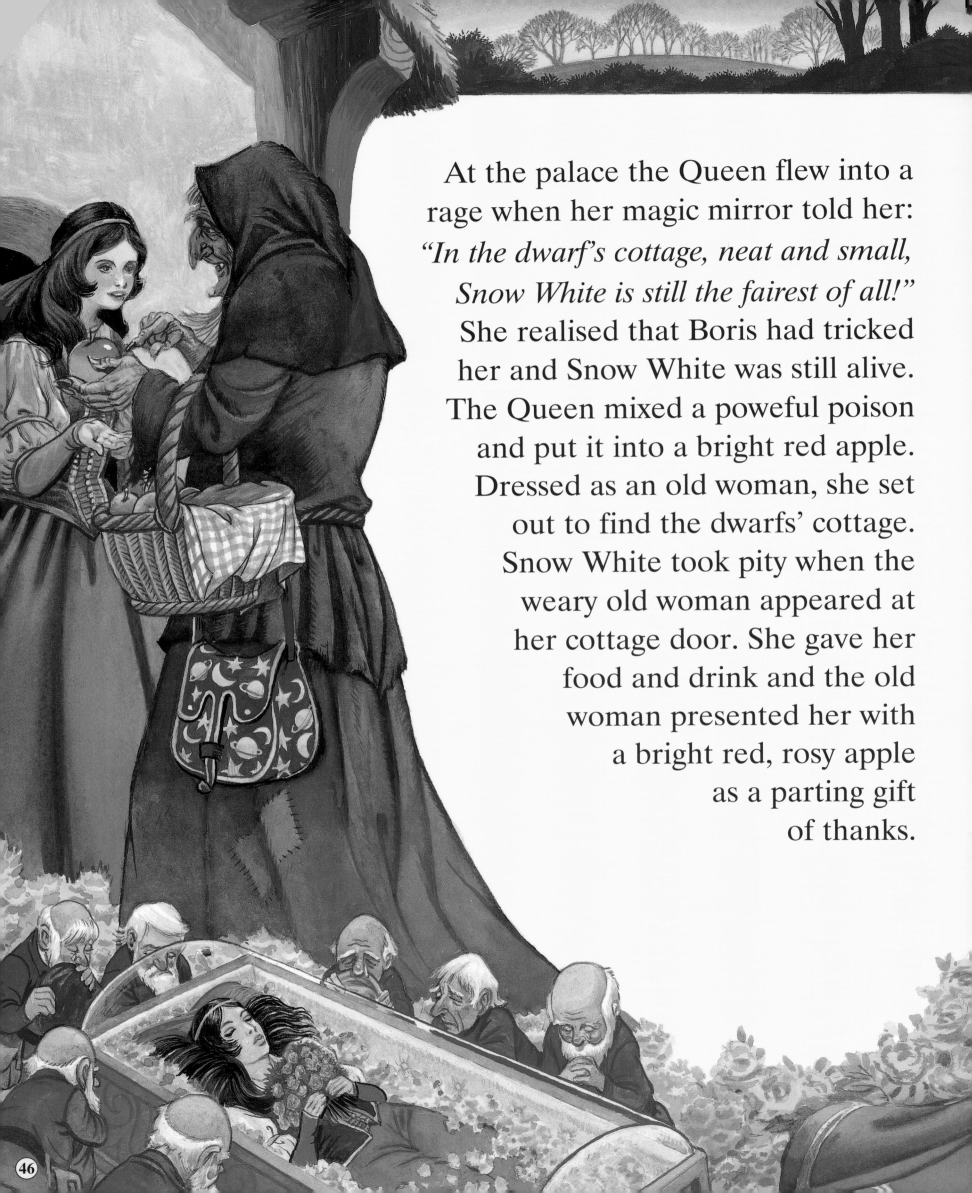

At the palace the Queen flew into a rage when her magic mirror told her: *"In the dwarf's cottage, neat and small, Snow White is still the fairest of all!"* She realised that Boris had tricked her and Snow White was still alive. The Queen mixed a poweful poison and put it into a bright red apple. Dressed as an old woman, she set out to find the dwarfs' cottage. Snow White took pity when the weary old woman appeared at her cottage door. She gave her food and drink and the old woman presented her with a bright red, rosy apple as a parting gift of thanks.

Snow White took a big bite from the rosy apple. Instantly, she dropped down dead! The Queen's poison had done its work. In a flash the old lady turned into the evil Queen and then into a wicked witch. This was her true form. Just then, the dwarfs returned and chased the witch away so quickly that she fell down a hole and was never seen again.

Sadly, the elves were unable to bring Snow White back to life. They placed her in a crystal glass coffin surrounded by the flowers she loved so well. Then one day a handsome prince rode by. He fell deeply in love with Snow White and stooped to kiss her frozen brow. Because it was a kiss of true love, Snow White was restored to life. She and the prince danced for joy. They married and lived happily ever after.

The Ugly Duckling

Mother Duck had six tiny ducklings. They ran around, soft feathers gleaming, all waiting for the last egg to hatch. Suddenly, there was a CRACK. The shell broke open. Out poked a head, a long neck and untidy brown feathers. 'WHAT an ugly duckling!' quacked Mother Duck.

'What an UGLY duckling!' the other ducklings quacked. 'Go away!'

Poor ugly duckling! Nobody wanted him. He swam across the lake and hid among the water weeds, where he stayed all winter.

Then, as the days became warmer, some white birds with long, slender necks glided by. The ugly duckling came out from behind the weeds, making the waters ripple. One of the birds turned its head. He waited for the bird to call out. 'Ugly duckling! What an ugly duckling!' Instead, the bird bent its

long, slender neck in greeting. 'Come and see!' it cried to the others. 'A new swan has arrived!'

'A – a swan?' stuttered the ugly duckling. 'What is a swan?'

'YOU are a swan!' said the bird. 'Just like us! Look in the lake and see for yourself!'

So, he looked, and instead of an ugly duckling, he saw a beautiful bird.

'See your lovely white feathers!' said the other swans.

'Your smooth back and your long neck. You ARE a swan!'

'A – a SWAN?' Even his voice sounded different. 'So, I was never an ugly duckling! I WAS a swan! I AM a swan!'

Then off he swam with his new family, the happiest swan that ever there was.

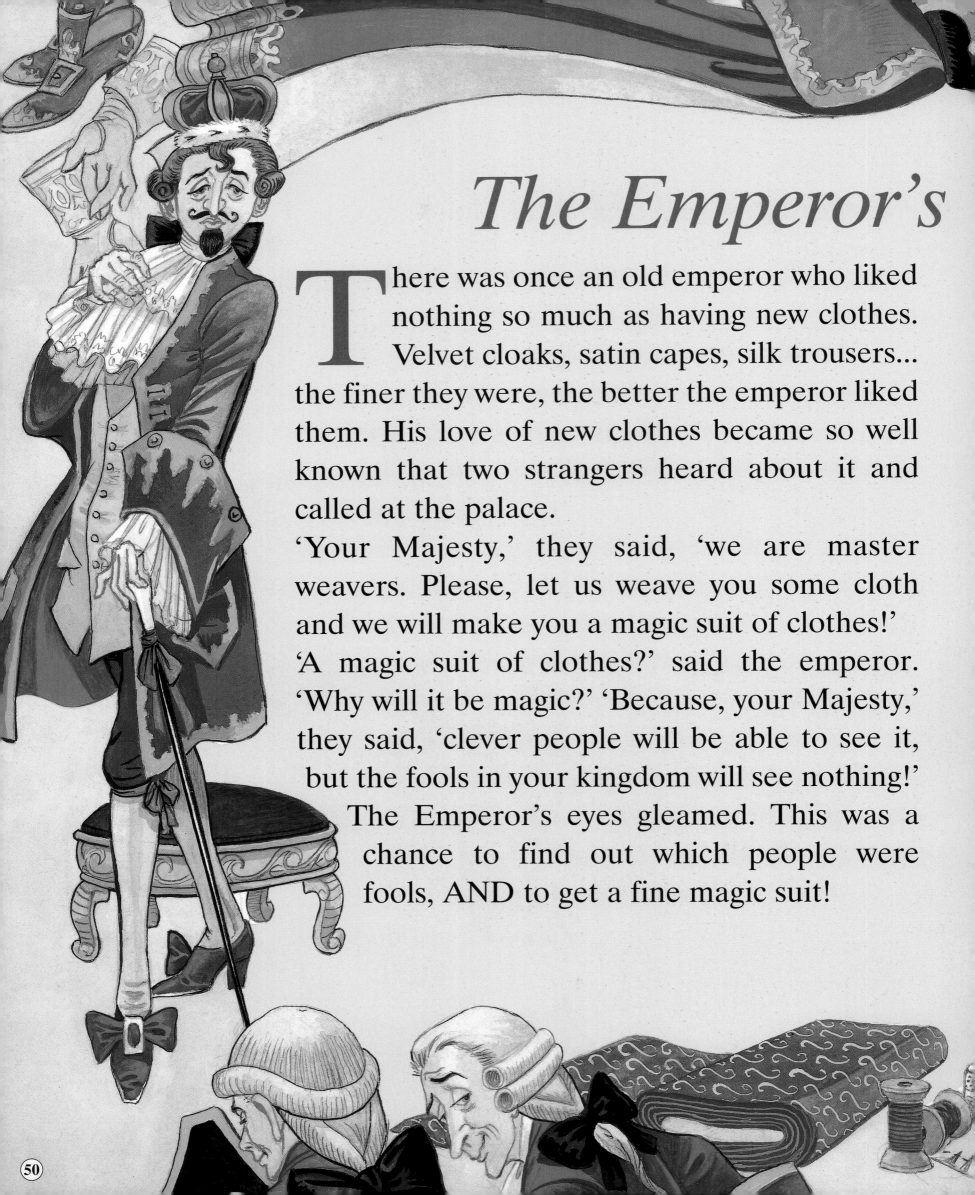

The Emperor's

There was once an old emperor who liked nothing so much as having new clothes. Velvet cloaks, satin capes, silk trousers... the finer they were, the better the emperor liked them. His love of new clothes became so well known that two strangers heard about it and called at the palace.

'Your Majesty,' they said, 'we are master weavers. Please, let us weave you some cloth and we will make you a magic suit of clothes!'

'A magic suit of clothes?' said the emperor. 'Why will it be magic?' 'Because, your Majesty,' they said, 'clever people will be able to see it, but the fools in your kingdom will see nothing!'

The Emperor's eyes gleamed. This was a chance to find out which people were fools, AND to get a fine magic suit!

New Clothes

'You shall have all the money you need!' he said. But the strangers were common cheats. The money that the emperor paid them, they put in their pockets. 'Prime Minister,' said the emperor. 'Kindly go and see how the weavers are getting on with my new clothes!' So the Prime Minister went to see the two men. 'Look at the lovely colours!' they said, pointing to their empty weaving looms. 'Pity the fools who cannot see our work!'

Of course, there was nothing to see! 'But if I say that I see nothing, I admit to being a fool!' the Prime Minister said to himself. 'So, I must pretend that I CAN see the cloth!'

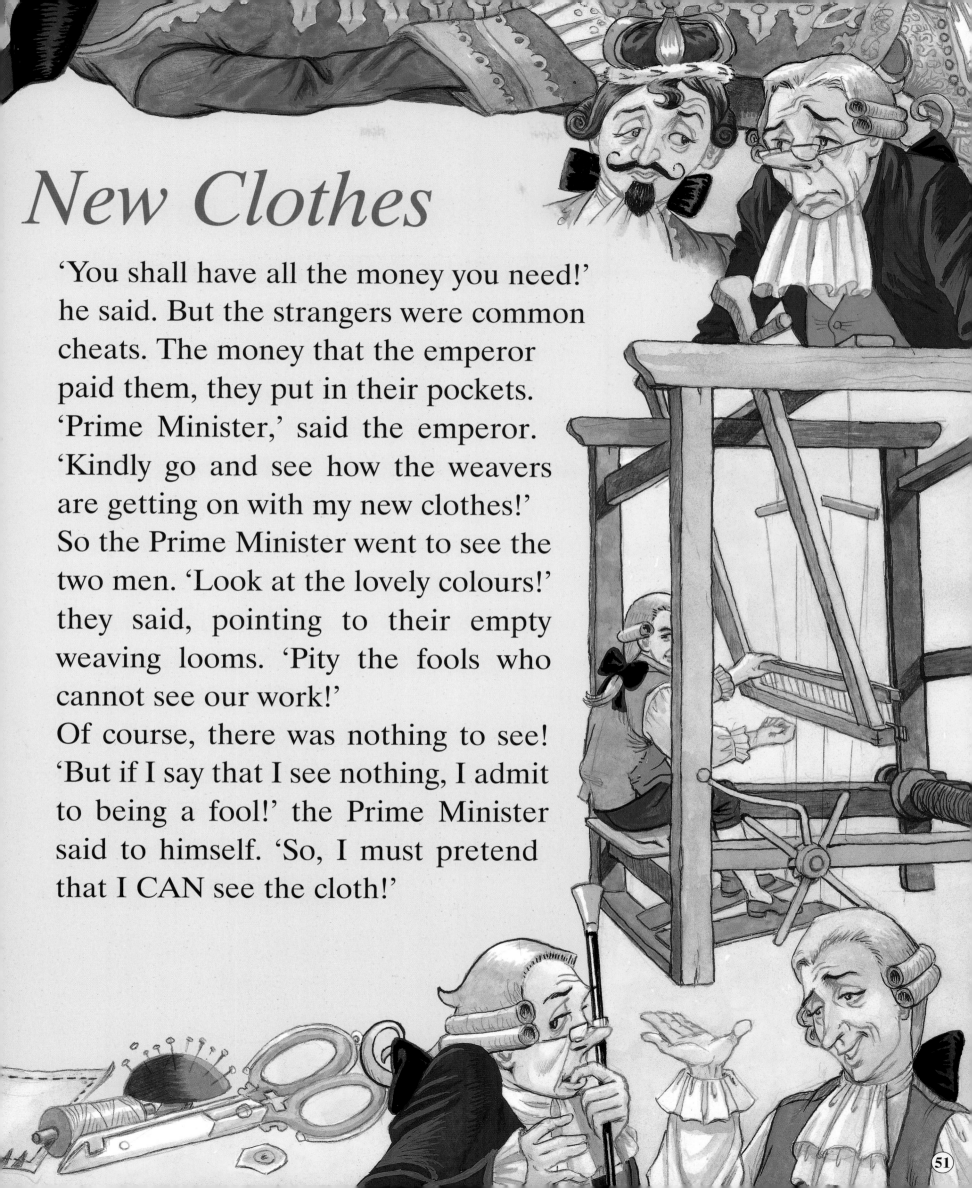

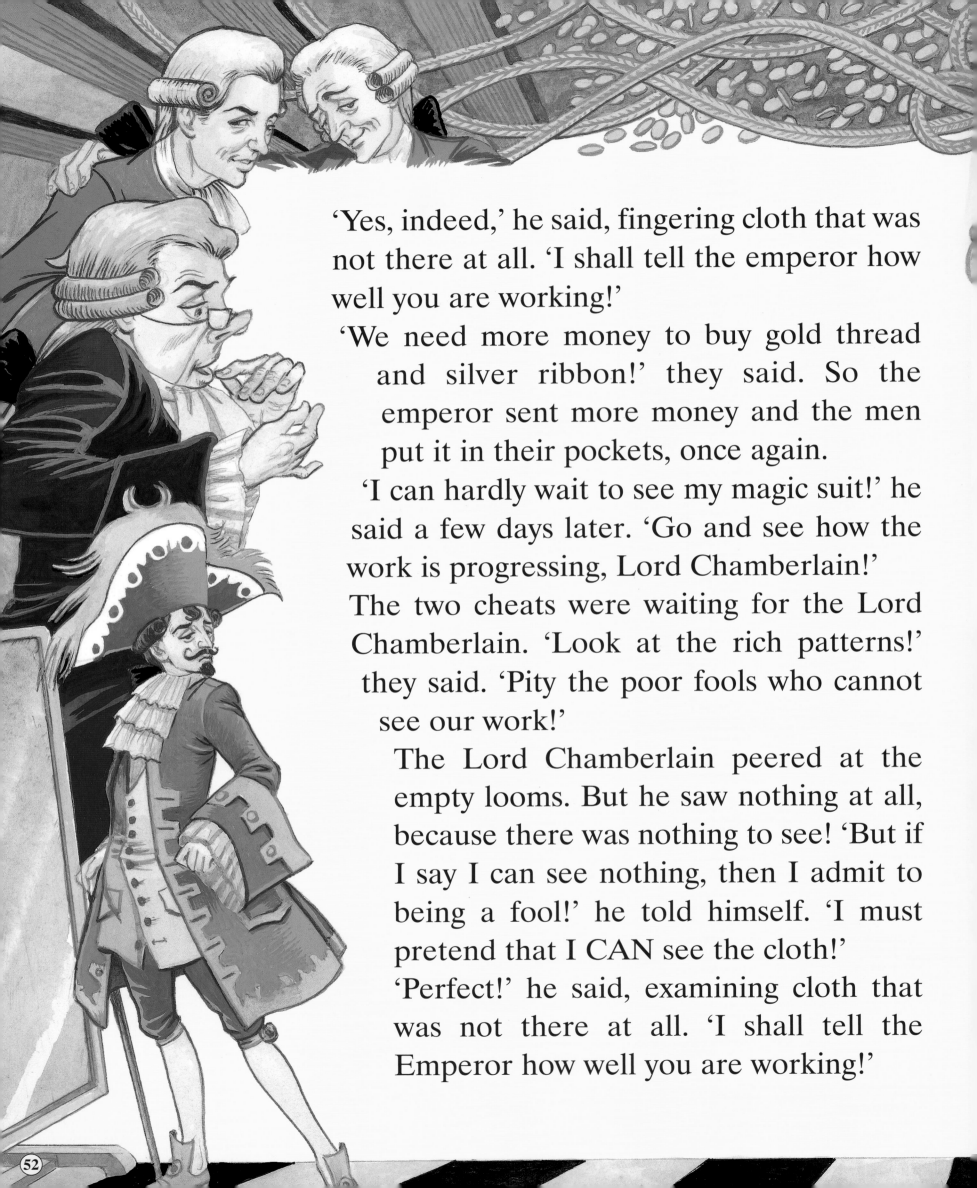

'Yes, indeed,' he said, fingering cloth that was not there at all. 'I shall tell the emperor how well you are working!'

'We need more money to buy gold thread and silver ribbon!' they said. So the emperor sent more money and the men put it in their pockets, once again.

'I can hardly wait to see my magic suit!' he said a few days later. 'Go and see how the work is progressing, Lord Chamberlain!'

The two cheats were waiting for the Lord Chamberlain. 'Look at the rich patterns!' they said. 'Pity the poor fools who cannot see our work!'

The Lord Chamberlain peered at the empty looms. But he saw nothing at all, because there was nothing to see! 'But if I say I can see nothing, then I admit to being a fool!' he told himself. 'I must pretend that I CAN see the cloth!'

'Perfect!' he said, examining cloth that was not there at all. 'I shall tell the Emperor how well you are working!'

'Tell him we need more money to buy gold braid and silver buttons!' they said.

'Well?' said the emperor when the Lord Chamberlain returned. 'Is my new suit of clothes nearly ready? What is it like?'

'Simply splendid, Your Majesty!' said the Lord Chamberlain. 'Such cloth! Such stitching! Just the gold braid and silver buttons to buy and I think it will be finished!'

'Good!' said the emperor rubbing his hands. 'Take this money to the weavers! Tell them I shall wear my new suit for the royal parade, next week!'

By now, everyone in the kingdom had heard about the magic suit of clothes.

'Such a fine suit!' said his page.

'The emperor will look magnificent!' said a footman.

'And it is a MAGIC suit of clothes!' added the royal cook. 'That means, only a fool will not be able to see it!'

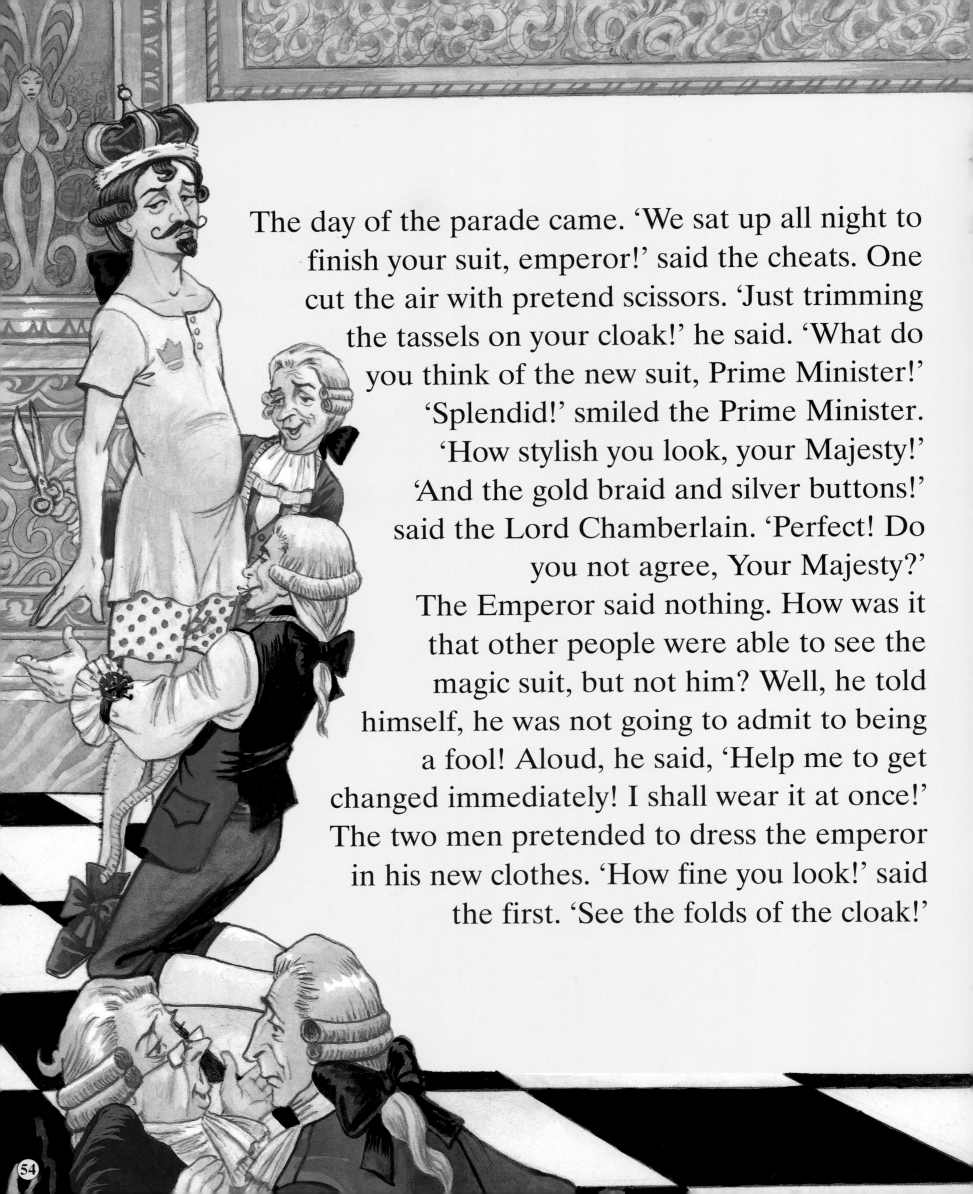

The day of the parade came. 'We sat up all night to finish your suit, emperor!' said the cheats. One cut the air with pretend scissors. 'Just trimming the tassels on your cloak!' he said. 'What do you think of the new suit, Prime Minister!' 'Splendid!' smiled the Prime Minister. 'How stylish you look, your Majesty!' 'And the gold braid and silver buttons!' said the Lord Chamberlain. 'Perfect! Do you not agree, Your Majesty?' The Emperor said nothing. How was it that other people were able to see the magic suit, but not him? Well, he told himself, he was not going to admit to being a fool! Aloud, he said, 'Help me to get changed immediately! I shall wear it at once!' The two men pretended to dress the emperor in his new clothes. 'How fine you look!' said the first. 'See the folds of the cloak!'

'And the perfect line of the trousers!' said the second man, pointing to the emperor's bare legs. 'Wonderful!'

Feeling rather cold in his under-clothes, the emperor stepped out under the royal canopy which was carried by four pages.

'See the emperor's new clothes!' said one lord.

'Such fine stitching!' murmured a princess.

The parade moved on. 'Look!' came a boy's voice. 'The emperor is out walking in his vest and pants! Ha-ha!'

'The simple voice of a child,' said an earl. But other people were laughing, too. 'Ha-ha-ha! So these are the emperor's new clothes! Ha-ha-ha!'

Now, everyone was laughing, including the Prime Minister and the Lord Chamberlain. How pleased they were to know that they were not such fools, after all!

The Little Match Girl

It was New Year's Eve. The snow had been falling all day. Nobody was about except for a little girl, hoping to sell matches. The little match girl crouched down between two houses with lights in the windows and the smell of delicious food drifting out into the cold air.

'A match might warm my hands,' she thought. She took one from her apron and struck it against the wall. As the little girl cupped her hand around the flame, she could see herself beside a warm stove. Then, the flame went out and the stove vanished.

She struck another match. Its light fell against the wall and it was as if she could see into a room, with a table set ready for a meal. Then the match went out, leaving only the damp, cold wall.

She lit another match. Now, she was under a Christmas tree with candles on its branches. The little match girl reached out towards them. The match went out, but she could see the bright, Christmas lights rising up and mingling with the stars. She struck another match. In the darkness she could see her grandmother. But her grandmother was dead. 'Grandmother!' she cried. 'Take me with you! When the match burns out, you will vanish like the stove, the food and the Christmas tree!'

She rubbed a whole bundle of matches against the wall. Brightness shone all around her grandmother as she took the little girl into her arms. 'Poor child!' people said next day when the little match girl was found, the burned-out matches beside her. 'She wanted to warm herself.' They did not see the smile on her face or know how happy she was.

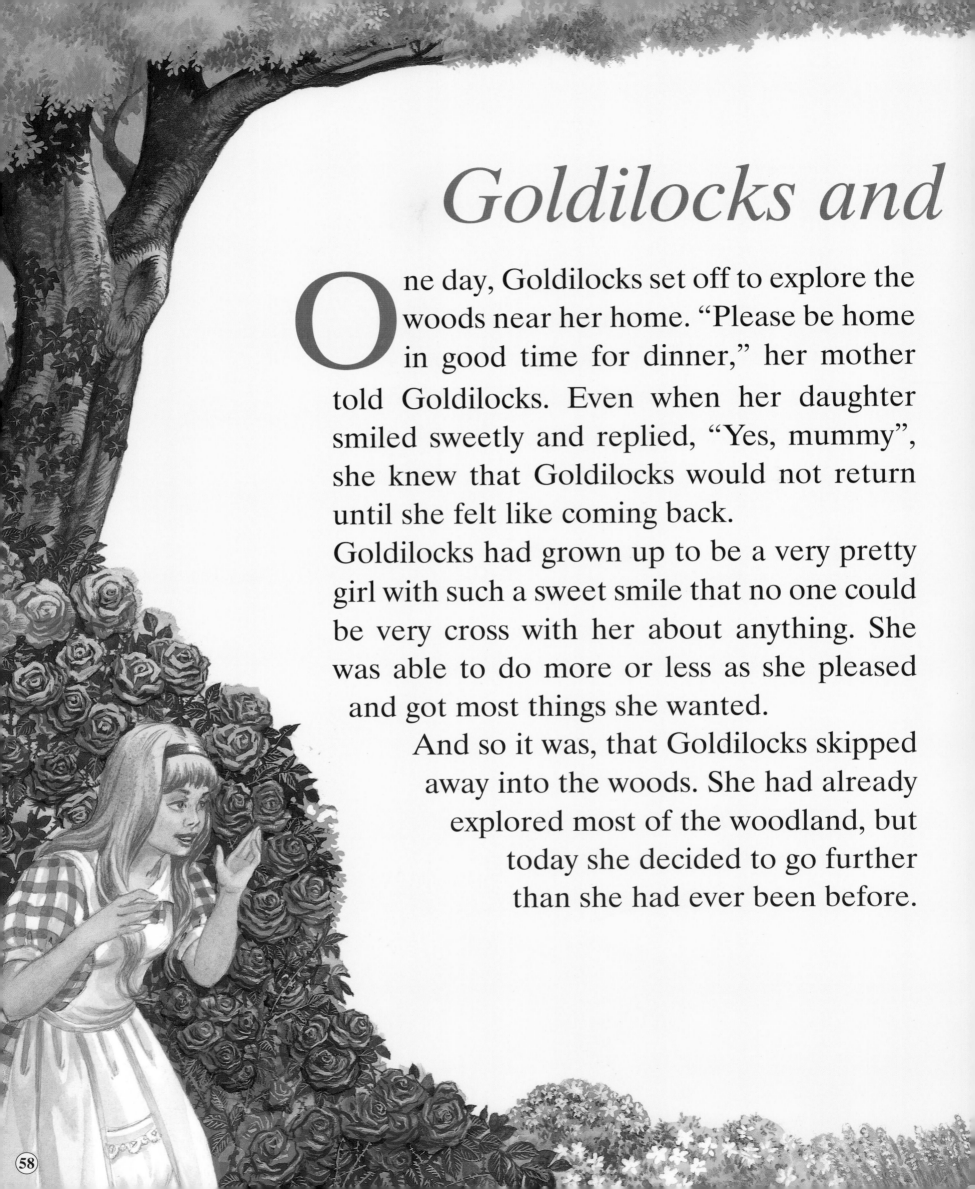

Goldilocks and

One day, Goldilocks set off to explore the woods near her home. "Please be home in good time for dinner," her mother told Goldilocks. Even when her daughter smiled sweetly and replied, "Yes, mummy", she knew that Goldilocks would not return until she felt like coming back.

Goldilocks had grown up to be a very pretty girl with such a sweet smile that no one could be very cross with her about anything. She was able to do more or less as she pleased and got most things she wanted.

And so it was, that Goldilocks skipped away into the woods. She had already explored most of the woodland, but today she decided to go further than she had ever been before.

the Three Bears

Goldilocks set off along a new trail and soon came upon a cottage almost hidden by the trees and bushes. It was a very charming cottage. There were pretty curtains at the windows and flowers in tubs by the door. The door of the cottage was open, so Goldilocks tapped gently on it and called out: "Hello – is anyone at home?" There was no reply. It was all very quiet. "I wonder who lives here?" thought Goldilocks. She had no idea that anyone lived in a cottage so near to her own home. Goldilocks stepped quietly through the open doorway into what was a large kitchen, or dining room.

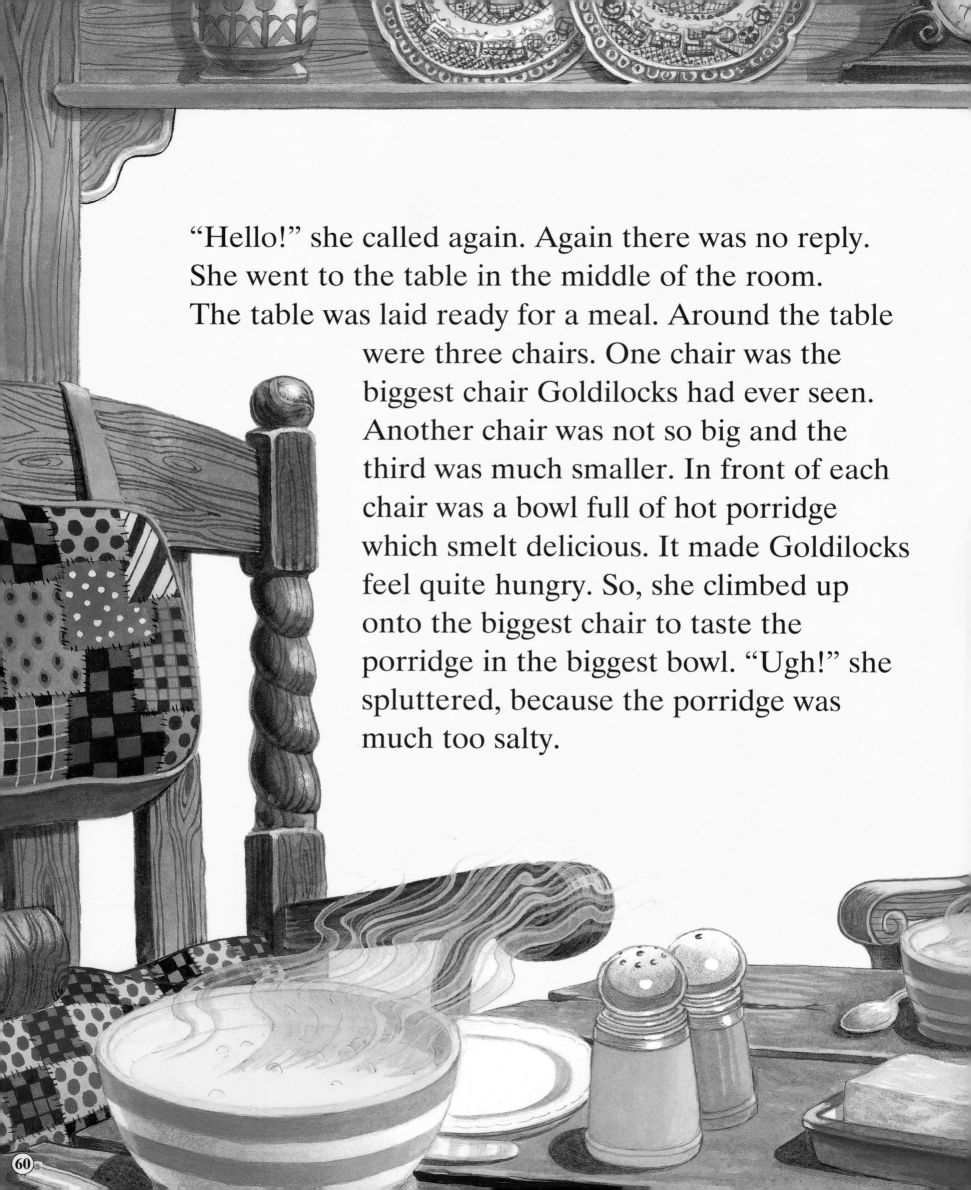

"Hello!" she called again. Again there was no reply. She went to the table in the middle of the room. The table was laid ready for a meal. Around the table were three chairs. One chair was the biggest chair Goldilocks had ever seen. Another chair was not so big and the third was much smaller. In front of each chair was a bowl full of hot porridge which smelt delicious. It made Goldilocks feel quite hungry. So, she climbed up onto the biggest chair to taste the porridge in the biggest bowl. "Ugh!" she spluttered, because the porridge was much too salty.

Next, Goldilocks climbed onto the middle-sized chair and tasted the porridge in the middle-sized bowl. "Arggh! Much too hot!" she cried out. Finally, Goldilocks sat in the smallest chair and tasted the porridge from the smallest bowl. "Hmmm! How good that is!" she thought. The porridge in the smallest bowl was not too salty, or too hot. It was just right. Without thinking about who the porridge had been made for, Goldilocks ate every bit and wiped the bowl clean. She still had no idea who lived in the cottage, but could have guessed if she'd seen the little family picture on the shelf above her head.

Goldilocks explored the rest of the cottage. In the bedroom were three beds. One bed was huge, another was middle-sized and the third quite tiny. Goldilocks suddenly felt very, very sleepy after her busy morning, so she tried each bed in turn. The smallest one was by far the best for her. She lay down and very soon fell fast asleep.

The bear family, who lived in the cottage, were on their way home. Mother Bear had gone out to call them in for breakfast just before Goldilocks arrived. When he arrived home, Father Bear roared: "Who's been sitting in my chair and tasting my porridge?" Mother Bear said: "Who's been sitting in my chair and tasting my porridge?" Baby Bear cried: "Who's been sitting in my chair and eaten up all my porridge?"

In the bedroom, Father Bear roared: "Who's been sleeping in my bed?" Mother Bear cried: "Who's been sleeping in my bed?" Baby Bear shouted: "Who's this sleeping in my bed?" All this shouting and roaring woke up Goldilocks, who was terrified at the sight and sound of the three angry bears.

The bears were so surprised at the sight of Goldilocks in their home that they just stood and watched in amazement as she fled from their cottage. In fact she didn't stop running until she got home, safe but very much out of breath. "Ah! What a good girl you are to run home trying to be in good time for dinner," smiled her mother. Of course, she didn't know the real reason Goldilocks had run all the way home!

so many led

so many de

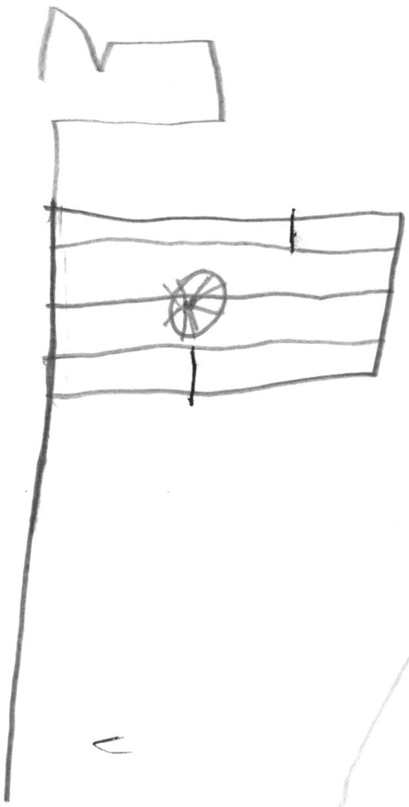

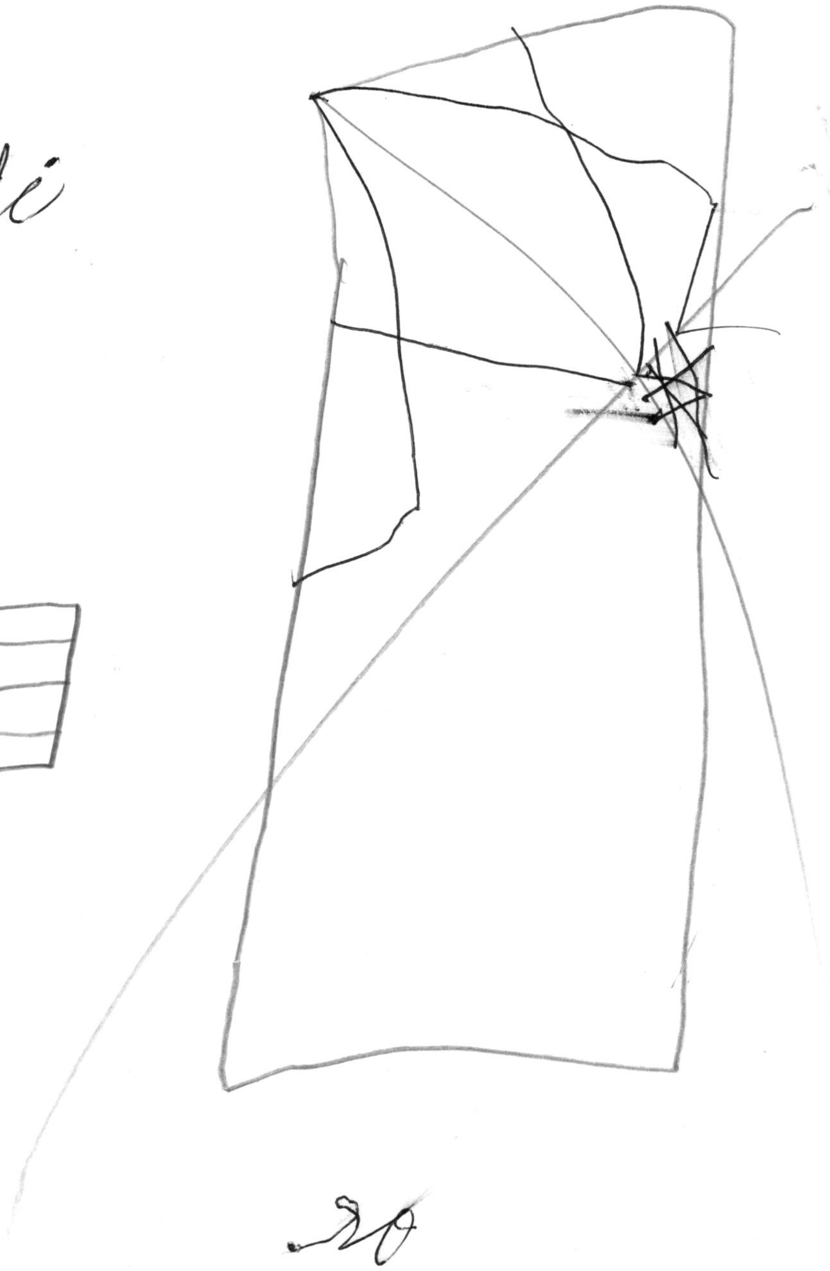

so

b

so

I saw many

Many flowers in my garden.

It should items

many flowers

in my garden

garden

garden

garden

Business
Quirinus Solutions Limited

Overdraft 40489254519
amount

fd 40359480433

Savings $

88924133

sort code - 608371

QUKI1030314

Rappechan Madassery
Variath

LI   11-04-98

02088906